# Through the Fire: An Alternate Life of Prince Konstantin of Russia

TAMAR ANOLIC

Copyright © 2018 Tamar Anolic
All rights reserved.
ISBN: 1725894866
ISBN-13: 978-1725894860

# CONTENTS

# ACKNOWLEDGMENTS

Two of the stories published in this collection have been previously published by literary journals. "Rumors of War" was published in *The Copperfield Review* in May, 2017. "Before the Fire" was published in the Spring, 2018 version of *The Helix*. Thank you to the staff of both journals for these publications- your encouragement has made this collection a reality.

Once again, thank you to my graphic designer, Bob Rubin. Your work is always of the highest quality.

Thank you to my friends and family, who have remained interested in reading these short stories since I started writing them.

Character List


Prince Konstantin Konstantinovich Romanov: Prince of the
        Imperial Blood, third son of the Grand Duke Konstantin
        Konstantinovich
Princess Pilar of Bavaria: Konstantin's wife
        Their children:
                Prince Sergei Konstantinovich
                Prince Boris Konstantinovich
                Princess Olga Konstantinova
                Princess Marie Konstantinova


Konstantin's family:
His parents:
        Grand Duke Konstantin Konstantinovich, the Imperial
                family's greatest poet
        Grand Duchess Elizaveta Mavrikievna
His siblings:
        Prince Oleg Konstantinovich
        Prince Igor Konstantinovich
                Princess Sophie of Hohenburg: Igor's wife
                        Their children:
                                Prince Peter Igorievich
                                Prince Nicholas Igorievich
                                Prince Oleg Igorievich
        Prince Ioann Konstantinovich
                Princess Elena of Serbia: Ioann's wife
                        Their children:
                                Prince Vsevolod Ioannovich
                                Princess Ekaterina Ioannovna
                                Princess Elizaveta Ioannovna
                                Princess Kira Ioannovna
                                Prince Vyacheslav Ioannovich
                                Prince Gleb Ioannovich
        Prince Gavril Konstantinovich
                Lady Maud, daughter of the Duke of Devonshire:

Gavril's wife
Their children:
Prince Nicholas Gavrilovich
Princess Anna Gavrilovna
Princess Tatiana Konstantinova
Prince George Konstantinovich
Princess Vera Konstantinova


Nicholas II: Tsar of Russia through 1920

Alexei II: son of Nicholas, tsar of Russia beginning in 1920
Princess Ileana of Romania, later Tsarina Ileana: Alexei's wife
Tsarevich Konstantin Alexeievich: Alexei and Ileana's oldest
son

# BEFORE THE FIRE

## Part I: First Impressions

A footman opened my carriage door, and I stepped out into the summer heat of Saxe-Altenburg, the German duchy not too far from home. In front of me, a tall white church stood proudly against the deep blue sky, and I had to squint into the sun to see the cross on top of it. Papa and Mama got out of the carriage behind me. The footman closed the door behind them, and the driver cracked his whip. The carriage drove off, its wheels creaking on the cobblestones.

I looked back at the church. Huge bouquets of colorful flowers had been set up on each side of the doorway. They were so redolent that I could smell them even at this distance. It was all very pretty, but I still felt out of sorts. Already, I missed Bavaria, with its wildflowers and tall, snow-covered mountains.

"Pilar, you look wonderful!" I heard someone say, and I turned to see Princess Olga of Hanover standing nearby. Princess Victoria Louise of Prussia and Princess Adelaide of

Schleswig-Holstein-Sonderburg-Glücksburg stood next to her. All three of them nodded and smiled at me.

"Thank you," I managed to say as Mama and Papa moved off to talk with someone else.

"I wish I had your coloring and fair hair," Victoria added.

I knew it was a compliment, and still I had to stop myself from making a face. I hated getting dressed up like this, and I never would have been comfortable in the more sophisticated, long-skirted dresses my friends were wearing. Much as I did not want to admit it, though, I did actually like the dress I was wearing, and with my hair woven back as it was, I could almost stand my reflection in the mirror.

All four of us looked at the church, then back at each other. It was obvious that we were uncomfortable about going inside. "I can't believe a Russian Grand Duke came all the way here to dedicate a church," Olga said.

"The Grand Duke Konstantin Konstantinovich," I said, stumbling, as I always did, over the second name.

"His wife is a princess of Saxe-Altenburg and they're dedicating this church to her," Victoria said. "Besides, this Grand Duke is one of the more religious ones in Russia."

"Know it all," I said, even if I said it with a smile.

Victoria shrugged. "At least he's here with some of his sons. Maybe I'll finally secure a good match and I won't have to listen to Mama and Papa whine about it anymore."

Adelaide nodded. "And the Russian Imperial family is certainly wealthy enough that they're all good matches."

I could almost agree with that. I still was unsure if I wanted to leave Bavaria forever, but if I had to marry into a foreign land, I would definitely prefer a wealthy prince to one who was barely scraping by.

"The oldest one is already engaged," Olga gossiped. "I can't imagine why he bothered coming here today."

"It isn't always about the marriage market," I said. "He's here because they're dedicating this church to his mother." *Keep ignoring the details, Olga,* I thought. *It'll serve you well in the future.* "Who's he engaged to, anyway?"

"Princess Elena of Serbia," Adelaide said. "I can't imagine what he sees in her."

"I think she's pretty," I said, but I could tell my companions didn't agree.

"He's probably concerned he'd never find a bride otherwise," Adelaide sniped. "The Grand Duke is handsome, but his sons are all so tall and thin and funny looking."

*And that is why you are still unmarried,* I thought, already tired of the gossip. "Shall we go inside?" I asked.

It was cooler in the shadows of the church than it had been outside, and I was grateful for that. The Grand Duke and his family were already in the chapel, obvious even at that distance because of their height. Maybe Adelaide had been right about that after all. The Grand Duke was distinguished looking, despite his advanced age, but he and his sons were all well over two meters tall. Even from across the chapel, I felt dwarfed.

For a few minutes, I watched the Grand Duke and his wife interact with the royals that had assembled to greet them. Six of their eight children stood behind them- five sons and one daughter, smiling and laughing. I tried to hide my nervousness by playing with one of the pamphlets that the church had printed for the occasion. The date on the top of the program- July 12, 1911- reminded me how far along I was in my life: twenty years old and still unmarried, with nary even a prospect. I took a deep breath. Perhaps today would change that.

Victoria, Olga, and Adelaide surrounded me, and I was glad for their company. Together, we eyed the Russian princes across the room. "Which is the one that just got engaged to Elena?" I asked.

"One of the taller ones next to the Grand Duke," Victoria said. "The two really tall ones are the oldest, but I can't tell them apart."

The Grand Duke and his sons all stood tall and proud in their immaculate uniforms. The confidence they exuded practically came across the church in waves. For the first time, I could see why people might be intimidated by them. *Maybe Olga, Victoria, and Adelaide are all intimidated, in addition to being as nervous as you are,* I told myself. *Perhaps that's why their chatter has an undercurrent of acrimony. You shouldn't be so short with them. Try to be more understanding.*

Just then, one of the slightly shorter Russian princes looked in our direction, and I could see how clear and pale blue his eyes were. They reminded me of the glass vase in my bedroom at home, which was a similar color. Even at this distance, his eyes were striking.

I swallowed. Which prince was that one, again? A couple of the princes had biblical names, another one had been named after the Grand Duke, and there were a couple more besides that… I couldn't remember which was which. I had spent several days trying to associate names with faces from the postcards of the family that the Russians were so fond of printing. I realized now how little my studying had helped.

"Pilar," Papa said from nearby, and when I looked at him, he tilted his head towards the front of the church.

I followed him and Mama, feeling dread rise up in me. I prayed that my shyness wouldn't render me completely unable to speak. Behind me, Olga, Victoria, and Adelaide joined their parents and also started moving forward to meet the Grand Duke and his family.

Papa kept a hand at my elbow as the Grand Duke's eyes focused on us. "Ludwig, Maria," the Grand Duke greeted my parents with a smile. Then he looked at me in particular. "And you must be Princess Pilar."

His German was perfect, and I was impressed.

"My only daughter," Papa confirmed, smiling. "Your memory has always amazed me, Your Imperial Highness."

The Grand Duke nodded. Then his eyes focused on me again- nay, his eyes seemed to bore into me. Instinctively, I fell into a curtsey. "It is a pleasure to meet you, Your Imperial

Highness," I said, relieved that my tongue didn't trip over his formal title. I sent a silent prayer of thanks upward.

"The pleasure is mine," the Grand Duke replied. He introduced his wife and children.

The one daughter that was with them was Tatiana. Her smile was warm and her light blue eyes twinkled. I liked her immediately. Upon hearing her brothers' names, I remembered that it was Ioann- the oldest- who had just gotten engaged to Elena. "Congratulations on your engagement," I said.

"Thank you," he said. "I am so happy." A genuine smile lit up his face, and I started to like him too.

Gavril was by far the tallest of the princes, and I felt even smaller standing next to him than I had at the back of the church. Adelaide had been right, though- he was so tall and thin, much like a reed. The prince with the pale eyes that reminded me of my vase was Konstantin, the one named for his father. Now that I was standing next to him, I could see that his eyes were so clear that I felt like I was looking straight into his soul. He held my gaze until I looked over at my mother, who was talking to Ioann.

"When is the wedding?" Mama asked.

"We're planning it for September," Ioann said, his grin still lighting up his face.

Mama smiled too. So did the Grand Duke. Ioann's happiness was contagious- to almost everyone, anyway.

"We should all be so lucky," Prince Konstantin said.

I detected a level of bitterness in his voice, and I looked at him uncomfortably.

"Kostya," the Grand Duke rebuked his son.

"Sorry, Papa," Konstantin replied. He rearranged his features into a more neutral expression.

I continued looking at him. His eyes captivated me. My ears, however, went to the gossips behind me. "He was hoping to marry Princess Elizabeth of Romania, but her parents wouldn't allow it," Adelaide whispered.

I sympathized with Konstantin, but I also felt embarrassed by Adelaide and her lack of tact. If I could hear her whisper, couldn't Konstantin hear it also? He was standing right in front of me, after all. But he gave no indication that he'd heard Adelaide, and I was relieved. *He must be more diplomatic than she is,* I thought.

After a minute of awkward silence, the church's priests began entering the chapel. "Should we begin the ceremony?" the Grand Duke asked.

Everyone nodded in assent, and soon my parents and I were moving towards the pews. The Russian princes took seats in the pews in the front of the church, on the left side as we faced the priests. My parents and I sat one section over to the right and a few pews back.

I gave the Russian princes one more glance as I settled into my seat and found that Konstantin had turned back to look at me. Once more, the pale blue of his eyes unsettled me. *He knows what I'm thinking,* I thought. *He can see straight into my head.*

Konstantin caught me looking at him and smiled. I smiled back. It was the first time that I felt the trip here from Bavaria was worthwhile.


Part II: Second Thoughts


Prince Konstantin Konstantinovich of Russia sat on a train, staring out the window as the train hurtled towards St. Petersburg. The bright yellow summer sunlight shone on the trees' heavy foliage, creating dapples of light on the branches and on the ground. Konstantin kept his eyes on the trees to avoid seeing the Russian Imperial double-headed eagle that seemed to be everywhere on the train- over the doorway, on one of the tables, even on the flask of fine Russian vodka that he held. *My rank and family mean nothing if they don't help me find a bride,* he thought. *Our peasants find love more easily than I do.*

Konstantin heaved a sigh. *At least we're going home now,* he thought. *I'm glad we honored Mama by dedicating that church, but I miss the Marble Palace.* He clenched his teeth. *It also hurts me to see how happy Ioann is, and how happy everyone else is for him. Besides, all of Europe now knows I was interested in marrying Elizabeth, and that I was rejected. No one else will ever be interested in me again.*

Konstantin took a swallow of vodka from his flask and inhaled deeply. The smells of borscht and kasha wafted over from the train's dining car. The borscht in particular was so fragrant that Konstantin could almost feel the silky concoction sliding down his throat. "Kostya?" he heard someone call, and he recognized Ioann's voice in the next car.

*Go away,* Konstantin thought. He stared resolutely out the window again as he heard Ioann, and then their brother Gavril, call his name again. Still, he ignored them. In a second, the door to his car slammed open, making Konstantin jump. He looked over as Ioann and Gavril entered the car, folding their tall bodies through the doorway. As the door closed behind them, they sat in the plush, upholstered seats across from Konstantin and fixed their eyes on him.

"Did you not hear us calling you?" Ioann asked.

"Of course I heard you," Konstantin said irritably. "I'm not deaf." The three brothers stared at each other for a long moment. "What do you want?" Konstantin asked finally.

"Papa was looking for you," Ioann said.

"Where is he?" Konstantin asked.

"In his compartment," Gavril answered.

"Is he feeling unwell?" Konstantin asked, genuinely concerned. *Father was in Germany for a month, taking a cure before we dedicated that church,* he thought.

"It's not about him, it's about you," Gavril said in his usual direct way. Ioann eyed Gavril with amusement before looking back at Konstantin.

"Great," Konstantin said unhappily, but he finally stood up and went to find their father. A few minutes later, he was knocking on the door of the Grand Duke's compartment, holding on to the door frame for support against the rocking of the train.

"Enter," the Grand Duke Konstantin ordered.

Prince Konstantin entered the compartment to find his father sitting with a book in his lap.

"Kostya, I was hoping that was you," the Grand Duke said, laying aside his book and standing. The rings on his long fingers sparkled in the sunlight that streamed through the windows. He swept Konstantin into a hug. Konstantin hugged his father back, but his heart wasn't in it, and he was glad to be released a minute later.

The Grand Duke gestured for his son to sit, and Konstantin settled into a comfortable armchair. The Grand Duke sat facing him, and his kind eyes searched Konstantin's translucent blue ones. "My heart hurts to see you in pain," he said.

Konstantin shrugged noncommittally. Unable to meet his father's gaze, he stared out the window. Outside, the scenery continued to fly by in a blur.

"Kostya, look at me," the Grand Duke said gently.

Konstantin looked back at his father. Tears gathered in his eyes and threatened to overflow. The Grand Duke reached out and took Konstantin's hand. His skin was soft against the top of Konstantin's hand, and Konstantin tried his hardest not to let his tears overflow in the face of his father's kindness.

"I know how hard it must be to get a negative answer to a marriage proposal," the Grand Duke said. "You were interested in Elizabeth for some time."

"What difference does it make now?" Konstantin asked, his voice rough with the sound of his unshed tears.

"I don't want to see your pain chase away other eligible brides," the Grand Duke replied.

"Is that why so many unmarried princesses were at the church today?" Konstantin asked, pulling his hand away from his father's and wiping his running nose with the back of his hand.

The Grand Duke handed his son a handkerchief as he answered the question. "That was a part of it," he said honestly. "Those families were there because of our rank, but also because you, Gavril, Oleg and Igor remain unmarried. Those other families are as interested in your prospects as I am."

"Igor is too young to marry- he's only seventeen," Konstantin replied as he made use of the Grand Duke's handkerchief. "Even Oleg is barely old enough."

"I'm not talking about having their weddings happen tomorrow," the Grand Duke said. "I just want all of you out there, meeting people."

Konstantin looked away and stared at the pile of books on the nearby table. *I'd rather be doing anything than having this conversation,* he thought. *Even reading those books, whatever they are.*

"Princess Pilar seemed nice," the Grand Duke said, trying to draw his son out.

Konstantin nodded as he looked back at his father. *She was pretty, too,* he thought. "I got a better impression of her than of the other princesses there," he said honestly.

"Did you know that she's exactly your age? Perhaps it's worth arranging another meeting with her."

"Please don't hurry me into anything, Papa," Konstantin begged. "I'm really not ready yet."

"I know that," the Grand Duke replied, reaching out and taking Konstantin's hand again. "But when you are ready, perhaps this is a path forward."

Konstantin nodded. *Perhaps,* he thought. *I'm not convinced yet, but I don't want to keep Pilar waiting forever either.*

The Grand Duke rose. "I need to get back to my books," he said.

Konstantin rose also and headed for the door, glad that the conversation was over. The next car was mercifully empty, and Konstantin took a minute to wipe his eyes and nose again with the handkerchief he was still holding. He took a few deep breaths and swallowed the lump in his throat.

Then, noticing that the setting sun was casting slanted rectangles of golden light across the floor of the moving train, Konstantin went to see if his brothers wanted to play a game of billiards.

# STOLEN CIGARETTES

The familiar ache had been growing in my chest ever since we left St. Petersburg. I needed a cigarette, and I needed one badly. I looked over at my older brother Ioann. We had switched seats for the carriage ride home, and he now sat next to my overcoat. "Would you hand me a cigarette, Ioannchick?" I asked. "There are a few in my coat pocket."

But Ioann shook his head. "Not anymore," he said. "Igor stole them on the way out of the carriage when we arrived at church."

"Damn him!" I burst out. "I'm going to have to label my cigarettes from now on- 'Konstantin's only- don't touch!'"

An amused smile graced Ioann's face as he turned to look out the carriage window.

My itch for a smoke was growing by the second. There would be cigars at our childhood palace of Pavlovsk, and we were headed there now, but those cigars were our father's. The long, thick cigars fit better in his hands than they fit in mine, and cigar smoke always infiltrated his clothing nicely. The scent also hung in the air long after Papa had stopped smoking, a sweet smell that managed not to be cloying. But the cigars never held the same wonder for me as they did for my father, so cigarettes it was- if I ever managed to get home and get my stolen smokes back from Igor.

When we arrived at Pavlovsk, Igor had already skedaddled inside, arriving home in front of me and Ioann because he'd gotten in the first carriage. *He knows I'm about to box his ears for absconding with my cigarettes,* I thought as I got out of my carriage. As soon as we were inside the Palace, I heard a noise just up the hall. I was certain it was Igor, and I was ready to take a bite out of him.

Instead, my younger sister Vera stuck her head into the long hallway from the nearest drawing room. "Ah, Kostya, you're back now too," she said. She came into the hallway. She had smile on her face and a doll in one hand. "Igor said to make sure I gave you these," she said, and held up a pack of cigarettes with her other hand.

I shook my head as I took them. "He's only being nice because he stole the last of the cigarettes I had in my coat."

"I know," Vera said, her smile widening into a grin. "He's sure he's about to get a beating."

"He's right," I said. Despite my frustration at my brother, I couldn't help but smile at my sister, so much younger that she was still a child. "So where is this wayward brother of ours?"

"I don't know where he went," Vera said.

"Well, I'm going to go find him," I replied, and headed for the staircase. It didn't take long- quick steps hurried down the hall as I approached the Palace's second story. "Igor!" I yelled, and the steps hurried away faster.

I dashed down the hallway and soon caught up with Igor, who had been racing into the safety of the apartments he shared with our brother George. Igor laughed as he tried to keep me out of his rooms by closing the door as fast as he could. But I was having none of it- I immediately shoved my arms out and managed to keep the door open.

"You stole my cigarettes!" I yelped. "Did I give you permission to do that?"

"If I'd had your permission, I wouldn't have needed to steal them!" Igor replied, still laughing.

I shook my head at him as I shoved the door open- no small feat, given that Igor was using all of his strength to try to keep me out.

"Didn't you get the pack I left with Vera?" Igor asked as we continued to shove at the poor door.

"I don't want that pack, I want the ones I had in my pocket."

"Too late!"

I finally managed to overcome Igor's resistance and shoved the door open wide enough to slither into Igor's rooms. Then I threw the package of cigarettes at him. The package hit his shoulder as he ducked to avoid it. "Damn you, Igor!" I yelled. "Do you know how badly I wanted a smoke on the drive home?"

Igor bent over and retrieved the wayward cigarettes from the floor. Then he opened the package, took one out, and put it in his mouth. "Want one?" he asked.

For a moment, I stood as if nailed to the floor, stunned by his sauciness. Then we both burst out laughing.

"Yes, I want one," I said when I could breathe again. He handed one over, and lit both of ours. Then I inhaled deeply once more, finally feeling the calming smoke reach my lungs.

# TRAINING FOR WAR

I could feel my boots pressing against my feet as we marched. Sweat poured down my face and body as my regiment moved towards Krasnoe Selo. Even my light summer uniform began to chafe against my body. *Great,* I thought. *I'm going to have blisters on my feet and red marks on the rest of my body.* Then I thought of the calendar in our regimental offices and remembered that it was already July, 1912. Where had the time gone?

Up ahead of me, I could see Major Daniltschenko, my commanding officer, leading the march. I looked behind me. The rest of my regiment dragged their feet on the ground, struggling to complete the march. "Move faster, men," I ordered them. "Krasnoe Selo is nearly in sight. We're almost finished."

The men closest to me gave me a weary look, and no one moved any faster. "It's too hot, Your Serene Highness," one of them said.

"I know it's hot," I replied. Didn't they see me sweating too? "But this is Russia- in a couple of months, you'll be complaining that it's too cold to march." I shook my head at the frustrated soldiers in front of me. "We don't get to choose our battlefields or our weather when we're fighting on them. The least we can do is train for what we'll get." I took a deep breath. "And please call me Captain Romanov."

*I hate being addressed by my imperial title,* I thought. *I just want to be a soldier.* I turned away from the men I'd been addressing and started marching again. I wanted to complete this march in good faith and I didn't mind using all of my strength to do so, but I would be glad when it was over- I had that much in common with the men behind me, at least.

I glanced over at Major Daniltschenko to find him smiling at me. "What?" I said. "I hope you're not smiling at the blisters that must be covering your feet as well."

Daniltschenko laughed as we struggled up another hill. "You've always set a strong example for the men, Kostya," he said. "And they respect you for it."

I just shrugged. Maybe he thought he was right, but I could never tell whether the men actually respected me, or whether they made sure to because of my title and rank.

I was relieved when the buildings of Krasnoe Selo came into sight a few minutes later. As we marched towards our barracks, I could see the Chevalier Life Guards Regiment returning from its own long march. My oldest brother, Ioann, marched at the front. *He'd be obvious anyway because he's so much taller than everyone else,* I thought, but it wasn't just that. *Ioannchick inherited our father's awareness of our title. He carries himself like a prince, and everyone knows it.*

I winced as I stepped down on the biggest blister that had developed on my foot. *I'm only aware of our title because no one will let me forget it,* I thought.

Ioann came to find me in the barracks just as I was removing my boots. He too was still sweating, and I was glad to see that he had been marching as hard as I had been. "Yuck," Ioann said as he watched me remove my socks and saw the oozing blister that had been giving me so much trouble. "You really should get that treated."

I couldn't disagree with him as I examined my foot. The blister looked like a bruise- purple and painful. I grabbed a nearby towel, some ointment, and some bandages as Ioann lowered his tall, thin frame into a seat next to me.

Ioann was silent for a minute as he watched me bandage my foot. Then he said, "so what's bothering you besides that blister?"

"Who said anything else was bothering me?"

Ioann glanced around and saw the number of soldiers from my regiment that were still surrounding us. Uneasily, he remained silent.

*This is my regiment's barracks, Ioannchick,* I felt like saying. *Were you expecting my soldiers to be somewhere else?* When I finished bandaging my foot, I looked back at him, and he jerked his head towards the door. Reluctantly, I stood up and followed him. Despite my medical efforts, I could still feel the blister every time I stepped down. I groaned.

When we were outside, Ioann repeated his question. "So what's bothering you, Kostya?" he said. "Even from where my regiment was marching, I could see that your frown was as dark as a thundercloud."

I gritted my teeth. "Was my dissatisfaction that obvious?"

Ioann nodded.

I sighed, suddenly feeling guilty for showing my emotions, and for not even being aware that I had been. "The men in my regiment don't work hard enough," I complained. "So many fall out during our long marches."

Now it was Ioann's turn to sigh. "These are the elite guards regiments," he said. "There are plenty of men who are only here because of their rank and lineage."

"Like us, Ioannchick?"

Ioann glared at me. "I work hard so that people don't think that of me."

"At least we're on the same page about one thing."

Ioann looked away briefly, and his angry expression lessened. "There are plenty of men who are here because their family expects it of them," he said. "Many would rather be doing something else. Try not to be so hard on them."

"If they want to do something else, then they should do something else," I replied without hesitation. "As long as they are here, they should work hard at being good soldiers and officers."

Ioann looked back at me, and a small smile made his lips turn up at the corners just a bit. "If everyone in our army shared your attitude, we'd have the best army in the world."

"There's no reason why we shouldn't have the best army in the world, Ioannchick," I said emphatically. "We are Russians, after all."

Ioann smiled again, a broader smile this time. He was about to reply when we both caught sight of three familiar figures coming towards us: the generals of both of our regiments and the distinguished figure of our father, the Grand Duke Konstantin Konstantinovich. *Papa must be coming to check on our training,* I thought.

Without even looking at each other again, Ioann and I snapped into salutes as our father and generals came closer. Papa smiled when he saw us, and I could feel pride seeping into every fiber of my body. Already, the pain from the long march had left my body, and my blisters were a thing of the past.

# RUMORS OF WAR

When Prince Konstantin Konstantinovich entered his father's study in the Imperial palace of Pavlovsk, he found his father standing at the window, staring out. It was April, 1914, and spring was just starting to find its way into St. Petersburg. The sunlight that flowed through the window was a pale light, but it was not as pasty as the Grand Duke Konstantin's countenance. Prince Konstantin sucked in a breath when he saw how ill his father looked.

The Grand Duke heard his son gasp and turned from the window. "Ah, Kostya," he said. He gestured for his son to sit. Konstantin settled into one of the comfortable chairs facing his father's desk, inhaling the smell of his father's cigars as he sat. "Are you still corresponding with Pilar of Bavaria?" the Grand Duke asked.

Sometimes, Konstantin wished his father didn't have such a good memory. "Yes, I am."

"And still no talk of marriage?" the Grand Duke pressed. "I thought you were interested."

"I am interested," Konstantin admitted. "And I told her as much."

"But?"

"*But* I've heard the same talk of war as you have. Some say Russia could mobilize her armies as early as next month."

The Grand Duke sighed. For a moment, he stared out the window again. Then he looked back at his son. "I don't think the mobilization will come that early, and yet my fear of war hangs over my head like an anvil. You realize that if Russia's armies moved across Europe, they would be marching against Germany? You and Pilar would be on opposite sides of the conflict."

The thought chilled Konstantin. "But if I brought her here as my wife, would that guarantee her safety?" he asked. "Or would it just leave her a very young widow?"

The Grand Duke did not have the time to answer before both he and Konstantin heard footsteps at the door of the study. A second later, Konstantin was glad to see his brothers Oleg, Igor, and Gavril come into the room. They took seats next to Konstantin, and the room was quiet as the four young men eyed their father, who continued to stand at the window, staring out.

Then Ioann, the family's oldest brother, slipped into the study, holding his four-month-old son, Vsevolod. The baby stared around with big blue eyes. A tuft of black hair stood straight up on his head. Finally, the Grand Duke turned from the window and smiled at the sight of his only grandchild. Ioann smiled back and hugged Vsevolod to his chest. The Grand Duke watched them for a minute before he held out his arms for the baby.

Ioann handed Vsevolod to his father and sat in the one remaining chair in the room. The Grand Duke sat at his desk and rested Vsevolod in his lap. Then he looked at his five sons and sighed. His pain was obvious. Konstantin felt himself tense up and saw his feelings mirrored in the anxious expressions on each of his brothers' faces.

"By now, you all have heard that Europe seems to be moving towards war," the Grand Duke said. "If it comes to that, I doubt Russia could avoid fighting."

Konstantin and all of his brothers nodded.

"But Nicholas himself doesn't want to go to war," Gavril said of the Tsar. "He thinks Russia has a long way to go before its railroads and other industries can support a war."

"I agree with him," the Grand Duke replied. "But the passions of our countrymen, and of our fellow Slavs, are running high. I'm not sure Nicky could keep Russia out of war, even if he were opposed to it."

"What about the Duma?" Ioann asked, naming the nationally elected congress. "The Duma has the final say over whether we enter the war. If both it and Nicky are opposed, perhaps Russia will remain neutral."

The Grand Duke shook his head, his disdain obvious. "The Duma consists of nothing but politicians that bend at the slightest wind," he said. "If people are clamoring for war, the Duma will make sure it happens, regardless of whether it's good for Russia." The Grand Duke shook his head. "The country needs strong men that stick to their principles, like Peter the Great."

"Nicky is no Peter the Great," Konstantin heard himself saying. "Peter could have kept us out of war. Nicky won't be able to." Everyone in the room looked at him.

Gavril in particular glared at his younger brother. "Are you disloyal to the Tsar?" he asked.

"I'm just saying what I see," Konstantin mumbled. Then he looked Gavril in the eye and spoke more clearly. "I am as loyal to Nicky as you are."

The room became silent, and Konstantin fancied he could see the tension in the air mingling with the sunlight that was still coming through the window. Then Vsevolod began to fuss, and Ioann stood up to take his son from his father. The Grand Duke did not object, but an intractable sadness filled his eyes. The expression remained there as Ioann took Vsevolod into the hall and handed him to his wife, Princess Elena.

From inside the study, Konstantin watched as Elena took her crying son and disappeared down the Palace's long hallway. "I'm sorry, Papa," he said as Ioann returned to the room and took his seat. "I didn't mean to upset you."

"It's not *you* that's upsetting me, Kostya," the Grand Duke replied. "It's the prospect having all five of you march off to war."

"And yet if my country calls, I can only reply," Oleg said, and Konstantin was grateful for his words.

The Grand Duke's eyes welled up with tears as he looked at Oleg. "You are the most talented, artistic and poetic of my eight children," he said. "Your loss in this war would be the greatest."

"Relax, Papa," Ioann said. "War hasn't even been declared yet."

"And yet I feel its rumble in my bones," the Grand Duke replied, standing and going back to the window. "We are headed down that path. All of Europe is."

Konstantin, Ioann, Gavril, Oleg and Igor looked at each other uneasily. Then Konstantin rose and joined his father at the window. "It will be alright, Papa," he said, putting a hand on his father's shoulder. "Truly it will be."

But Konstantin's reassurances were of little use. He watched his father's jaw clench and unclench. Then, despite the Grand Duke's efforts to the contrary, tears ran down his face. "Five of my sons marching off to war," he said. "I should never have lived to see this day."

# THE GREATEST PAIN

It was the end of September, 1914, and I had been fighting in the trenches since the war had started three months earlier. I was at the front, but we were only just starting to see some action. I was glad to finally engage the enemy- I'd felt almost useless these last couple of months. I raised my binoculars to my eyes and kept my gun firmly at my side. All around me, the men of my Regiment, the elite Izmailovsky Regiment, raised their guns.

Then I felt a hand on my shoulder. "Your Serene Highness, may I have a word?" someone said.

I glanced behind me to see Mikhail, a messenger, standing at attention. "What is it?" I asked, wishing that he hadn't used my formal title. Here at the front, I just wanted to be known as Captain Konstantin Konstantinovich Romanov.

"Major Daniltschenko wishes a word with you."

"Now?" I asked. Couldn't Misha see that we were about to come in contact with Germans? I wanted nothing more than to fight.

"He said it's urgent," Misha replied, looking at me uncomfortably.

I didn't like his expression. Reluctantly, I left my position and went to find Daniltschenko.

A few minutes later, Daniltschenko eyed me gravely as I snapped into a salute. "Your Serene Highness, I am sorry to be the one to have to give you this news," he began.

I looked down and saw a telegram in his hand. Instantly, my stomach sank and my heart began to race. Four of my brothers were fighting at the front. Something had happened to one of them, I was sure of that. "What's the problem?" I asked, unsure if I wanted to hear the answer.

"Your Highness' brother was wounded in action and has died of his wounds," Daniltschenko said. "I'm so sorry."

I collapsed into a nearby chair. "Which brother?"

"Prince Oleg Konstantinovich."

"Oh no, not Oleg!" I cried. He was the smartest, most talented of all of us. My father's favorite son. Tears ran down my face.

"I'm so sorry," Daniltschenko repeated. He put a hand on my shoulder as I used my own hand to wipe away my tears.

"I didn't think he'd be injured, let alone killed, this early in the war," I said.

"He was acting bravely, chasing and capturing a German patrol."

That meant little to me. I wanted my brother alive. I gathered my belongings and went to join the rest of my family in its grief. I managed to meet my family's procession on the way to Ostashevo, the country estate at which Oleg would be buried. Many members of the family joined our sad procession: my parents, of course, my uncle Dmitry, and the rest of my siblings. Only my sister Vera was absent- my parents thought that she was too young to attend the funeral. I disagreed. Vera was eight years old already and grieving too, but my parents' decision stood.

On the cruel morning of October 3, the train carrying my brother's body slowly made its way into the station nearest Ostashevo. It was a cold, windy day. Tears stung at my eyes as the chill in the air stung the rest of my body. The station was decorated with flowers and a black bunting. Many delegations had come to meet us- members of our household and quite a few others. Beyond the military guard of honor, over a thousand peasants stood waiting as well, their heads bared in respect, despite the cold.

The clergy prayed as we exited the train. My father and Dmitry helped me and my brothers carry Oleg's metal casket from the train to the waiting gun carriage. Then we followed the casket to the cemetery on foot. Oleg's favorite horse followed us in the procession as well, covered in black, with my brother's boots placed backwards in the stirrups. The wind remained so bitter and powerful that Dmitri looked stooped as he leaned into it.

The procession was silent as it moved, and it was only with great difficulty that I managed not to break that silence with my sobs. Even so, my tears continued to fall from my eyes. I looked at the sorrowful faces of the rest of my family, and could see all of them crying as well.

At the cemetery, prayers were intoned, and Oleg's coffin was lowered into his grave. I took a handful of soil to drop over the coffin, and the black soil crumpled against my fingers. I dropped the handful of it into the grave, and it clanged against the top of the metal coffin with a loud *thwack*. I winced. I hadn't meant to *throw* the dirt, just to *drop* it. Each handful of soil that the rest of my family threw made the same noise, however, and a dagger ripped through my heart at each sound. When the ceremony finally ended, we made our way back to our family's palace at Pavlovsk.

In the days that followed, my father seemed to have lost his will to live, and I feared for him. I remembered his fear, even before the war started, of having us all march off to battle. The memory haunted me, and I wished I could do more to comfort him. But, as usual, all words failed me, and soon the front was calling me back. As a Russian soldier, I could do no more than put my uniform back on and make preparations to leave the Palace. Papa nodded at me when I entered his study to say goodbye. "It is your duty," he said. "Go."

With those wise words ringing in my ears, I departed. As the train pulled out of the station near Pavlovsk, heading back towards the front, I felt an emptiness settle over me. I would never see Oleg again, and my heart hurt for the absence.

That tragedy was followed by another. Mere months after Oleg's death, word came to the front that Prince Bagration, my sister Tatiana's husband, had also been killed in action. To make matters worse, the continued fighting meant that his body could not be returned to Petrograd, and he was buried somewhere near where he was killed. Once more, I had to sit down as I received the news. Then I called Tatiana, and tears rolled down my face as we spoke.

Tatiana had so longed for her marriage, and her voice was rough with pain as we talked. All around me, I could hear machine gun fire as I strained to hear what Tatiana was saying. Then the telephone line went dead, and I was left holding a useless device. I could no longer hear my sister's voice, and I had nothing left to say. Still, I clutched the telephone until my knuckles turned white, as if I could bring Bagration back by sheer force of will.

It was late May by then. Not only had spring come to the front, but the fine weather also held the promise of the coming summer. Yet still my heart was cold. Slowly, I picked up my rifle and returned to the trenches. The weight in my chest made the short journey a long one.

I spent the next two weeks at the front. I dodged bullets, lead my regiment against the Germans, and thought that the worst of the news from Petrograd was over. I was wrong. In early June, 1915, just as the wretched heat of the summer was starting in earnest, Major Daniltschenko called me in one more time. This time, I simply eyed him, unable to fathom what the horrible news would be.

Seeing my expression, Daniltschenko handed me a telegram. "I'm sorry," he said- again.

I felt the paper in my hand, and braced myself for which of my other brothers had been killed in action. Would it be Ioann? Would he, like Prince Bagration, leave a widow and two young children? I took a deep breath and read the telegram. To my horror, it wasn't any of my brothers that had passed away this time- it was my father, whose long illness had finally gotten the best of him. I let out a string of curses that made even the soldiers around me blanch.

Once again, I gathered my belongings and made the long journey back to Petrograd. As I rode, I stood staring out the train's window, unseeing, unfeeling. Once more, I remembered my father's fear that all of his sons would march off to war, and that Oleg in particular would be killed. All of that had come to pass, and more.

Despite the length of my journey, I was the first of my brothers to make it back to the capital from the front. It was only then that the irregularity of our wartime transportation system really sunk in. Russia had been doing her best to industrialize in the years before the war, but she certainly remained behind countries like Great Britain and France. To make matters worse, the bombs and soldiers of our German enemies had done their part in demolishing what little gains Russia had made.

Inside Pavlovsk, I greeted my mother, who was barely able to contain her tears. Then I laid my belongings down in my old rooms and went to find my siblings who were still in the Palace- Tatiana, who had returned there with her children after Prince Bagration's death, and our two youngest siblings, Vera and George. At twelve years old, George was much too young to be fighting at the front. I hoped that the war would be long over before he came of age and could enlist.

I found George and Vera at one of Pavlovsk's many windows, looking out. "Watching for Ioann, Gavril and Igor?" I asked them.

They nodded wordlessly and continued looking out the window.

"So what happened to Papa?" I asked after a pause.

Vera and George looked at each other, then back out the window. Another silence followed. Finally, Vera spoke. "His heart problems again."

George continued staring silently out the window. "Talk to me, Georgy," I beseeched him. His silence was unnerving.

"Because you, Ioann, Gavril and Igor were at the front, George had to go tell the Tsar of Papa's death," Vera said.

I put my hands on George's shoulders and turned him around to face me. "Is that true?" I asked.

He nodded, and tears started to fall from his eyes.

"I'm sorry," I said. I pulled him to my chest and put my arms around him. After a minute, I could feel his shuddering sobs. When I looked out the window, I could see the rest of my brothers arriving at the front of the palace- Gavril and Igor first, followed by Ioann and Elena. Ioann was holding little Vsevolod, only a year and a half old, and Elena was heavily pregnant with their second child. *She can't have more than a month or so left in her pregnancy,* I thought, heaving a sigh.

On June 7, my entire immediate and extended family gathered in the palace's Italian Hall for the funeral's requiem mass. Then Papa's coffin was carried down the Palace Staircase, through the Egyptian Vestibule, and into the courtyard. Out in the courtyard, a gun carriage waited to carry the casket to the train station, where a funeral train would carry it into Petrograd proper.

As the coffin was conveyed to the carriage, I felt my heart sinking. I felt regret at the pain in which my father had spent the last few years of his life- not only the physical pain of his illness, but also the pain he'd felt at the last two of our family's deaths. I also felt regret in the ways that I could have been a better son. Why hadn't I done more with my life while my father was still alive? Tears stung at my eyes.

At the Nicholas Station in Petrograd, the coffin was placed into another gun carriage and drawn through the streets of the capital. Multiple guards of honor surrounded the coffin as my brothers and I followed it on foot. Tsar Nicholas II himself, as well as the family's Grand Dukes, also joined our sad procession on foot. My mother and the other women of the family followed us in closed carriages.

As we marched, I looked over at my brothers. Ioann and Gavril's tears were flowing down their faces, and Igor's face was twisted. I didn't feel any better. All around us, thousands of people had gathered along the route the funeral took to pay their respects, and the lines stood four or five deep. When we reached the Cathedral of the Fortress of Saints Peter and Paul, the coffin was placed on a bier where it would stay the night. Four poles surrounded the coffin and supported a canopy of black crepe. The poles themselves were covered with gold brocade, complete with gold fringe. Above it all, white ostrich feathers waved softly in the light breeze.

All of it drove home my father's status as a Grand Duke of the Imperial Family, as well as his status as a beloved poet and respected member of the military regiments in which he'd served. I was more aware of my own pain, however, and I had half a mind to spend the night in the Fortress to guard the coffin. Yet, when my family left, I went with them.

The next day, the burial service seemed interminable, and I began to feel exhausted. To my shock, my mother barely showed emotion throughout it all, and I couldn't believe that she wasn't as pained as the rest of the family. As the service ended, however, Mama approached Papa's coffin, and as the lid was slowly drawn over the body, she bent down. *What is she doing?* I wondered. Then I realized that she was trying to see Papa's face for as long as she could. It was only then that I knew my mother was feeling as much sorrow as the rest of us-her thirty-one year marriage had just ended, and yet she was young enough to be able to look forward to many years of life without my father.

The coffin was carried out the side door and down into the Grand Ducal vault, where it was lowered into its final resting place. My eyes burned and felt dry at the same time, and yet somehow my tears continued flowing. When the service ended, Ioann put one arm around Elena and one arm around our mother. Gavril put his arms around George and Vera as Vera held Tatiana's hand. Igor dropped his arm around my shoulders as we followed the rest of the family out of the Fortress. Gratefully, I returned my younger brother's embrace.

The day after the funeral, the Tsar himself visited us at Pavlovsk. His only son and heir, Alexei, had come with him, and Alexei's large blue eyes showed his sadness. "I'm very sorry about all of this," Nicholas told us. "Konstantin was one of my favorite cousins."

I could tell he was being honest. Both Nicholas and Alexandra had trusted my parents and let me and my siblings into their inner family circle in ways that few of our other cousins enjoyed. After he'd shared a few more words with my mother, Nicholas turned back to me, Ioann, Gavril and Igor. "Are you all headed back to the front in a few days?"

My brothers and I nodded. "What's your sense of the progress of the war?" I asked, now that I had Nicholas' attention. "Do you think it will end soon?"

Nicholas sighed, and he seemed weary. "No, I fear our armies are in for a long battle," he said.

That was the last thing I wanted to hear, and none of my brothers looked happy either. Two days later, I began my long journey back to the front- back to the fire, where the fighting might last indefinitely.

The clattering of the train rocked my body as I rode, but I was barely aware of it. Instead, all I could feel was the numbness that enshrouded my entire being. The train continued to move forward as night descended on Russia, entombing both the train and the scenery around it.

# HAUNTED

I felt my body rocking back and forth in the darkness as the train clattered across the tracks. Slowly, I came awake, and even more slowly, I sat up. *Where am I?* I wondered. But looking out the window provided me with no clues- all I could see were birch trees speeding by in dappled light. Grass and fog covered the ground, but I saw no familiar landmarks, no helpful hints. I could have been anywhere.

Slowly, I rose from my cot. My body felt like lead, heavy and unresponsive. I looked down and realized that I still wore my uniform, and the cot that I had been sleeping on was the same one I'd gotten used to sleeping on at the front. Yet, my gun was nowhere to be found. I looked around the train car and saw that it was the sparse transport car that the Russian army used to transport us soldiers. It was very different from the Imperial train to which my family- cousins to the tsar of Russia- was accustomed.

Taking a deep breath, I raised my head and looked out the window again. We were passing through a station without stopping. I went to the window, hoping for a written sign that would tell me where I was. Nothing of the kind greeted my gaze, but I was given a far more rewarding sight- my father, the Grand Duke Konstantin Konstantinovich, stood on the platform. My brother Oleg stood next to him. They were waiting for me, I was sure of that, and I smiled.

"Papa!" I called. "Oleg!"

Papa turned and looked at me, and I waved furiously from the window. But Papa, though he clearly saw me, made no move in my direction. Oleg didn't even turn to look at me. Instead, he stared straight ahead as the train continued to pass him.

The train, which hadn't even slowed down, raced out of the station. "Wait!" I yelled. "Papa! Oleg!"

*    *    *

Prince Konstantin Konstantinovich jerked awake to the sound of bombs and bullets. His breath came in ragged gasps, and he put a hand to his chest.

Nearby, another officer, Vladimir Nikolaievich Voronov, remained lying on his cot but turned to look at Konstantin. "Are you alright, Kostya?"

Konstantin took a deep breath, trying to get a sense of his surroundings. When he was sure he was awake, and he remembered that he was fighting the Germans in the Great War, he nodded. "I think so."

"I was wondering whether I should wake you," Vladimir continued. "You were twitching for a few minutes before you woke up."

"Bad dream, I guess," Konstantin replied.

Vladimir sat up. "What were you dreaming about?" he asked.

"My father and brother."

"Which brother- Oleg? The one that was killed at the beginning of the war?" Konstantin nodded, and Vladimir sighed. "I remember when that happened, and when your father died soon after. They were both good men."

Konstantin nodded again and stood up. When he was sure that he was steady on his feet, he turned and went to the window. *It's been almost a year since Papa's death,* he realized. *But*

34

*the hole that he and Oleg left is still there.* He took a deep breath as he thought of his father's long illness, which had only worsened in the months after Oleg's death. *Papa died more quickly because Oleg was gone. Why wasn't I good enough to keep him alive? I'm the one that was named after him.*

A lump formed in Konstantin's throat, and he choked back his tears. *It wasn't just about you,* he told himself. *You still have six siblings who are alive, and Papa couldn't keep himself alive for them, for his four grandchildren, or for Mama.*

Konstantin watched the distant fires for another minute, listened to the whine of bullets nearby. *So many deaths, and all for what?* he wondered. *We declared war in August, 1914. That means we've been fighting for nearly two years now, and all for what?*

Konstantin clenched his teeth. *So many wasted lives,* he thought, *and the fighting isn't even over.*

# HIDDEN LETTERS FROM MY BELOVED

We spent the day in the trenches, under a hail of German bullets. German bombs came at us, too, their aim increasingly deadly. But we Russians can shoot as well as the Germans can, and our bombs inflicted casualties upon our enemies too. When night fell, we had moved our position forward a few versts, and inflicted more losses on our enemy than we had received.

Our reinforcements came, and my men and I slipped back to safety to rest. "Kostya," I heard someone say. When I looked up, Vladimir Nikolaievich Voronov, a major in my regiment who had become a good friend of mine, was coming towards me. "These letters are for you," he said, handing me a stack of envelopes. "It looks like they're from your family."

"Thank you," I said, and I gratefully took the letters. The one on top was from my older brother Ioann, and was addressed to me with my formal title- Prince Konstantin Konstantinovich Romanov. *Ioann was always aware of our rank*, I thought, trying not to roll my eyes. *We're fighting at the front, not hiding in our palaces. We're as equal to the men around us as we're going to get.*

Still, I was happy that he'd written, and, in his spidery handwriting, he told me how blessed he felt to still be alive after two and a half years of fighting. "We'll probably be spending yet another Christmas at the front, though," he wrote.

*He wrote that more than a month ago, and it's clear now that he's right,* I thought. *It's December, and Christmas is less than two weeks away.* I shook my head. *Christmas, 1916,* I said to myself. *Where has the time gone?*

The next letter in the pile was from my mother, and her beautiful script made me picture her sitting at her desk at Pavlovsk, decorative pen in hand. Still, her missive expressed her concern for me and the three of my brothers that were still fighting at the front. "There have been shortages of food here in Petrograd, and reports of shortages at the front have caused protests and disturbances in the streets," she wrote.

I frowned as I read that. We had been dealing with shortages at the front for some time, it was true- shortages of rifles, bullets, and boots. Before the war, Russia had been building new factories at the behest of ministers such as Stolypin and Witte, but it seemed we could never produce enough. Still, we were making the most of what we had, which included supplies and soldiers from the United States, and our armies had recently begun to push the Germans back.

The next part of Mama's letter worried me even more. "Many people here in the capital are starting to blame the monarchy for the army's woes," she wrote. "Popular opinion is against Empress Alexandra in particular, calling her 'the German woman,' as if she's our enemy."

I bit my lip. Mama, too, had been a German princess before her marriage to my father. Could she be in danger as well?

"To make matters even worse," Mama's letter continued, "Rasputin disappeared last night, and many of us- especially Alexandra- fear the worst."

By now, I was biting my lip so hard that I drew blood, which ran down my chin. Cursing, I wiped it away and pressed my sleeve my lip to repair the damage. Rasputin was the *starets* that Alexandra had always relied on to cure Tsarevich Alexei's ills. What would happen to Alexei now if Rasputin couldn't help him? What would happen to Alexandra? Her own health had been declining along with Alexei's.

But I also felt torn. I had never liked Rasputin. His cold blue eyes always chilled me through and through, and his behavior was not befitting someone who dealt with Their Majesties- his drinking and orgies were legendary. Yet, Alexandra had always been adamant about keeping him around.

I leaned up against the wall next to my cot and stared out the dirty window in front of me. The shortages, the protests, Rasputin's disappearance- none of this could end well. I struggled not to feel sorry for myself, but I couldn't help it. Here I was, risking my life every day to save Russia from being overrun by the German army, and it was possible that none of it would make a difference.

Taking a deep breath, I read the rest of my mother's letter, which finished with two sentences about enclosing a letter from Princess Pilar of Bavaria, which was addressed to me but had been sent to Pavlovsk. "I think Pilar was smart to send the letter to you here rather than at the front," Mama wrote. "Given the general mood, if you were seen receiving letters from Germany, you could be suspected of being a spy."

I threw down the letter in disgust when I read that. A member of the Imperial family, spying against Russia? That would never happen.

"Everything alright over there, Kostya?" Vladimir asked from nearby.

"Yes," I said immediately, even as I continued to stare out the window.

"I've never seen you get so upset over mail from home," Vladimir continued. "Most of us are pretty happy to hear from our family."

"It's not that," I said as I turned to face him. "My mother has been writing of unrest in the capital. It's not an easy thing to read about from so far away."

Vladimir nodded. "My family has been saying the same things," he said. "Luckily the Tsar has some wise ministers and is still committed to working with the Duma. Maybe it will all straighten out for the better."

His words improved my mood ever so slightly, and I picked up the envelope that had contained Mama's letter, hoping that Pilar's letter was still inside. I was rewarded with another slip of paper. I smiled. Pilar's missives had always comforted me. My brother, my brother-in-law and my father had all died within a year of each other at the start of the war, and Pilar had written to me after each tragedy. It was one of the few things that had kept me going.

Even now, though, her letter was aware of the same danger that Mama's letter had emphasized. "It pains me that I have to send this letter through the Palace rather than directly to you at the front," she wrote. "But I fear to put you in danger in any way."

I clenched my teeth, and I could feel my tears rising in my eyes. It should never have happened like this. I had known Pilar for three years by the time the war had broken out, and had been contemplating marriage even then, but I simply hadn't pulled myself together to propose. If I had, she would at least have been safely in Russia now.

With a chill, I remembered a conversation I'd had with my father in the months before the war had begun. He had warned me even then that the fighting would put me and Pilar on opposite sides of the conflict. Once it had become increasingly clear that war was on its way, however, I had been too scared to marry- scared that I wouldn't survive the war, scared of having a German wife whose loyalties would be questioned or whose family and countrymen could be killed by our armies, even by my own regiment.

I wrapped my coat around me as I continued to shiver. I thought of Ioann, who had gotten married around the time I had met Pilar, and who had had his first child several months before the fighting had begun. *He still marched off to the front despite all of that,* I thought. *And he's had a second child since the war began.*

I stared out the window as snow started to fall outside. All around me, the men of my regiment were either writing letters to their families or sleeping, but I could not bring myself to do either. *Maybe I'm doing this wrong,* I thought, feeling lonely despite the letters that sat behind me, some of which were still unread.

I watched as a single snowflake landed on the window in front of me and slowly melted. Then I took a deep breath. I had no idea how much longer this war would last, or whether I would survive its hail of bullets and bombs. *But if I do make it,* I promised myself then and there, *I will marry Pilar and bring her back to St. Petersburg with me.*

# AT WAR'S END

I stood shoulder to shoulder with the men of my regiment. The cold November air cut into our skin as we clutched our rifles. Each of us wore heavy coats over our uniforms, and yet still we were cold. My coat had been new back in 1915, and now, three years later, it was worn out but it was all I had. Shortages at the front made me glad I had even this much. Plenty of soldiers actively fighting the enemy had even less.

I glanced down the line of soldiers of the Izmailovsky Regiment- my regiment- and felt pride swell my heart. Each of the men that surrounded me had proven themselves in battle, over and over again, against a formidable foe. So many of our comrades had perished in the fight against evil that there was not a man among us who had not known some deeply personal loss. In my case, it was my brother Oleg who had been felled by his wounds- the only member of the Russian Imperial family to be killed in this long battle. His loss stung at my very being, and I nearly wept at the thought of his not being here to see the war end. The subsequent deaths of my sister's husband and my father also meant that I would be returning home to a very different world.

With great difficulty, I brought my mind back to the present. My soldiers and I were at the western front, and it wasn't just our regiment. Other elite Russian regiments were mingled in with the American soldiers with whom we had been fighting for months now. I had never met an American before fighting with these soldiers, but they are a brave lot, and I have been honored to fight with them.  Our lines were still a good 700 versts from Berlin, but if the fighting ended before we reached the German capital, I would not complain. I had seen enough of the war's atrocities. I was ready to go home to St. Petersburg, and sleep in my family's warm palace.

I stared front again. None of us moved as we stood at attention, waiting to hear the latest news. For months now, we had been pushing the Germans back, and in the last few weeks, all of Germany's allies had begun to surrender. The end of the war was near, I could feel it in my heart.

Then, finally, Colonel Daniltschenko, my commanding officer, raced out with a telegram in his hand. "Germany has signed the Armistice!" he yelled. "The war is over!"

Instantly, we all burst into cheers. Many of us threw our hats into the air. The only difference between my regiment's celebrations and those of the Americans around us was that our cheers were in a hearty Russian, while the Americans were shouting in a lusty English. We were all howling the same thing, though. We had defeated the enemy. We were going home.

It was only later, as we were making preparations to travel away from the front, that Colonel Daniltschenko sought me out in particular. "Kostya," he said. "The tsar has distributed a list of men to whom he will be giving the Order of St. George."

My heart skipped a beat at the mention of one of Russia's top military honors, given only for bravery in battle.

"I think you should see this list," Daniltschenko continued, and handed me a piece of paper.

Halfway down the list of names, I could see my own name written in clear letters- Prince Konstantin

Konstantinovich Romanov. I could see the names of my brothers above and below mine- the names Gavril, Ioann and Igor stood out as if in red ink. It was confirmation that they all had survived the war. My stomach turned with happiness, and my heart flip-flopped in my chest. "Thank you, Colonel," I said. My humble response did not express my high gratitude at the news, but I've never been a man of words.

Daniltschenko seemed to understand me anyway. "It's my pleasure, Kostya," he replied. "Your bravery throughout this war is well recorded, and all of the officers and men like you very much."

Two weeks later, my men and I crowded into a train to begin the journey back to St. Petersburg. Despite the cold outside, the train car quickly became hot and stuffy. As we travelled, I smelled a combination of leather from our boots, some cabbage and black bread that someone had managed to obtain, and tobacco from the cigarettes we all smoked. It was a very Russian smell, and I almost felt at home, despite how far we were from our homeland. The train was moving slowly through the wet snow, and yet our pace did not bother me. I wasn't simply on leave this time- the war was over, and I would not be returning to the front.

That first train only took us as far as Lvov before it ran out of fuel. As soon as we disembarked, hurrahs greeted our ears, and all around me, I could see more Russian soldiers who were also waiting on the platform for the next train. Suddenly, I recognized the uniforms of the Chevalier Life Guards Regiment among the waiting soldiers. My heart skipped a beat. My oldest brother, Ioann, belonged to the Chevalier Life Guards. Immediately I made it my business to find him. It wasn't that difficult a task- Ioann is not as tall as Gavril, but his height still made him stand out from the soldiers around him.

"Ioannchick!" I howled. He heard me immediately, but he couldn't find me as quickly. I could see his head turn, saw his eyes quickly scan the mass of soldiers around him. "Ioannchick!" I cried again, waving my arms.

Then he saw me, and we pushed through the crowd of soldiers to reach each other. "Kostya!" he yelled as we struggled through the snow and the soldiers. When we finally reached each other, we hurled our arms around each other—and promptly slipped on the icy snow beneath our feet. In a second, we were both on our rear ends in the snow, but we were both laughing uncontrollably. Military decorum be damned.

Slowly, we managed to pull ourselves to our feet. The deep snow and icy conditions didn't help us much, but when we were both standing, we made our way into the station proper, where we hugged each other more safely. "It is so good to see you," I said.

"Not as good as it is to see you," Ioann replied. "I am really happy to be going home."

"Have you heard anything from Gavril or Igor?" I asked.

"Not in a couple of months," Ioann said, shaking his head as we both lit cigarettes. "I sure hope they're alive."

"They are," I said, and I told him about seeing all of our names on the list of recipients of the Order of St. George.

"I didn't hear about that," Ioann said, his eyes lighting up.

When the next train came into the station, we boarded along with our regiments and continued talking. "I'm looking forward to getting back to my regular life," Ioann said. His eyes misted over. "Two of my three children were born during this war, and I haven't even met the youngest one yet."

"Elizaveta," I said. Ioann nodded. "I had to hear about her birth when I was at the front one night."

"Me too," Ioann said, and real tears started gathering in his eyes. "It's no way to live."

I clapped him on the shoulder. "The war's over now, Ioannchick," I said. "We won't be living like this anymore."

"You sure that kid's yours?" a nearby soldier teased my brother.

"I had leave from the front at an appropriate time before she was born," Ioann replied, looking almost amused. "I'm not worried about it."

I was definitely amused by the conversation, but I agreed with Ioann. *There's no way Elena would be unfaithful,* I thought.

We stood like that for hours on the moving train, so packed in that we couldn't even sit. After awhile, my feet started to hurt, and yet I found the strength to ignore my pain. I was going home. A ghost of a smile remained on Ioann's face, and I'm sure my lips were slightly upturned as well.

We passed the border into Russia long after the sun had set. All around us, the blackness of the long winter night prevailed. Suddenly, a loud bang tore through the sky, followed by another, and another. All of the soldiers on the train ducked. We were being bombed, I was sure of that, and from Ioann's stricken expression, I knew he was thinking the same. I turned and looked out the window, hoping at least to catch sight of the bombs that were going to end my life.

Instead, I saw fireworks tearing through the sky. "Look!" I yelped. I pointed towards the window as the fireworks produced balls of all colors across the black ink of the night sky.

The soldiers around me all looked upwards, and their faces were lit up with different colors. "That must be in celebration of the war ending," Ioann said from behind me. "I'll bet we can expect more of that when we get home."

He was right. We entered St. Petersburg like heroes. Screaming crowds greeted us at the train station, thronging the streets. Tsar Nicholas himself, hearing that Ioann and I were on our way back, was at the train station with Alexei, his heir. Ioann and I snapped into smart salutes when we saw them. Our regiments followed suit. When the Tsar released us, he hugged us and welcomed us home. Alexei stood, saluting, and then shook our hands.

I dove into the arms of my sisters and mother as Ioann howled, "Elena!" I looked over at him in astonishment. Since when could he yell that loudly? But he had already scooped his wife up into his arms and was hugging her tightly to his chest. She was so much shorter than he was that that her feet barely touched the ground. I laughed at the sight.

In a second, little Vsevolod, nearly five years old, and Ekaterina, only three years old, were throwing themselves at Ioann and crying, "Papa!"

Ioann picked each of them up with one arm and spun around in circles as he held them tightly. Both children burst into laughter, and my brother kissed each of them. Then he put them back on the ground and went over to the pram that our mother had been rocking. I went with him and looked over his shoulder as he slowly bent over and pushed away the blankets to examine his newest arrival. Elena stood nearby, watching quietly.

Ioann reached out and lifted his tiny daughter from the pram. Her little face and small features were perfect. Ioann snuggled her to his neck as tears rolled down his face. "She's beautiful," he said to Elena. Then, continuing to hug the infant, he put his back to us and walked away a few steps, seeking some privacy with this child he'd never met.

For a minute, I watched him go. Then I danced in circles with my sisters Tatiana and Vera, laughing as I became increasingly dizzy. It was so good to be home. "Have you heard from Igor and Gavril?" I asked them.

"Just by telegraph," Vera said. "They're on their way home too."

"Hallelujah!" I said. I was looking forward to that reunion already.

# AFTER THE FIRE

It was evening in the Marble Palace. The dinner dishes had been cleared from the table in the formal dining room, and most of Prince Konstantin Konstantinovich's family was in the main hall, decorating the Christmas tree. *I've spent the last four Christmases at the front, and the Great War has only been over for a month,* Konstantin thought. Still, he felt compelled to be in the Palace's library with a number of open books in front of him. *I can help with the decorating tomorrow.*

He took a deep breath and inhaled the smell of old parchment. The deeper he breathed, the more Konstantin thought he could smell his father's cigars, which had been the Palace's dominant smell until the Grand Duke's death three years earlier. *If Papa were still alive, he'd be in favor of me marrying Pilar,* Konstantin thought. *Then I wouldn't up here, researching whether our Fundamental Laws allow it.*

All of a sudden, a pair of hands grabbed Konstantin's shoulders. Konstantin jumped in fright, gasping as he leapt. Behind him, his brothers Gavril and Igor burst into laughter. Konstantin leapt to his feet and spun around, nearly knocking over his chair as he did. "Damn you two!" he yelped.

"Oh, come on Kostya," Igor said. He leaned over the book that Konstantin had been reading. "The rest of us are downstairs, decorating the Christmas tree, and you're up here reading…. our Fundamental Laws?" His brow creased in disbelief.

Gavril, too, leaned over the stack of books on the table. Then he looked back at Konstantin. "What's bothering you, Kostya?" he asked.

"Who said anything was bothering me?" Konstantin replied. "Who even asked you two in here, anyway?"

Gavril and Igor looked at each other. Then they looked back at Konstantin, and each of them grabbed one of his ears. In a second, they were pushing his head back and forth.

Konstantin screeched in pain and pushed his brothers away. "What's the matter with you?" he yelled.

Gavril and Igor laughed again. Then Gavril put his arm around his younger brother's shoulders. "I'm serious, Kostya," he said. "Leave the books alone for tonight. Come and help us with the tree."

Sighing, Konstantin blew out the candles around the books and followed his brothers downstairs.

The next morning, the pale winter sun was barely over the horizon when Konstantin found himself in the library again. He had only been there a few minutes when Ioann folded his long body into the armchair next to him. Konstantin looked over at him and groaned. "Can I not get any peace around here?" he asked.

"Gavril and Igor said you'd be in here," Ioann replied. "What is it you need to research?"

Konstantin frowned. "The War toppled the whole of the German monarchy," he said. "I was wondering if Pilar of Bavaria would still be considered an eligible princess for marriage if she may not even be a princess anymore."

A wave of despair rode over Konstantin, and Ioann strove to reassure him. "So many of our family's brides have been German," he said. "Mama is German. I doubt all that will simply disappear as if it never existed."

"It just did, Ioannchick," Konstantin said. "The Kaiser abdicated, and Russia and our allies are working out a scheme of government to impose on the country. That's the end of it."

"Maybe not," Ioann said. "I rather think that they would be treated the same way the Bagrations were- as a former ruling dynasty. Tanya's marriage to Prince Bagration was considered equal because of it."

Konstantin shook his head at that. "The marriage wasn't considered equal, remember? It was a huge debate, but in the end, Nicky issued a ukase saying it wasn't, and Tanya had to renounce her succession rights."

"Perhaps we can convince Nicky to act differently this time," Ioann said. "Plenty of former dynasties, such as the French one, are still considered equal for marriage purposes."

"None of this would have been an issue if I'd just married Pilar before the War," Konstantin sighed. "I should have just done it then. I'm a bad person. She'll never accept my proposal."

"That's not even remotely true," Ioann said. "You're a Prince of the Imperial Blood, the recipient of the Order of St. George, and you've distinguished yourself fighting for our country to defeat a foreign enemy. Not too many other men can say that."

Finally, a small smile crept through Konstantin's gloom. "Thanks," he said.

"So why didn't you marry Pilar before the war, or even ask?" Ioann asked as he stood up.

"I told her I was interested. But when the war became imminent, I knew I would be going to the front. She deserves to be a wife, not a widow."

Ioann put a hand on his brother's shoulder. "Did I mention that you are noble, too?" he said, smiling. "Let's talk to Nicky. I'm sure he'll approve of this marriage, and think it's an equal one."

When Konstantin and Ioann met with Tsar Nicholas II in his study two days later, Nicholas was already mired in plans for the Peace Conference in Paris to settle the questions of the Central Powers' surrender from the Great War. When Konstantin and Ioann were led in, Nicholas was studying a map of Europe. His only son and heir, Alexei, stood next to him, bursting with excitement.

Alexei grinned when he saw his cousins. "I'm going to Paris with Papa for the Peace Conference," he said.

Konstantin smiled in return. "I'm glad you're looking forward to it," he said.

"So, what can I do for you, Kostya?" Nicholas asked as he sat down at his desk. Konstantin and Ioann sat in chairs across from him, and Alexei sat at a small table nearby to continue studying the maps.

Konstantin and Ioann looked at each other, and it was Ioann who spoke first. "Your Imperial Majesty, Kostya is interested in marrying Princess Pilar of Bavaria."

Nicholas nodded at the suggestion. "Your father mentioned that some years ago," he said. "When I heard nothing more, I assumed you had dropped the matter."

"It had more to do with the war intervening than my lack of interest," Konstantin replied.

"I can certainly understand that," Nicholas said. "My oldest daughters, too, would have married a few years ago but for the war."

Ioann leaned forward. "Your Imperial Majesty, what is your view about whether this would be an equal marriage?" he asked.

"Our father considered it to be equal before the war," Konstantin said hurriedly.

Ioann rested his fingers on Konstantin's hand, and Konstantin took it as a gesture to keep quiet. Both brothers looked at Nicholas for an answer.

"We're in a whole new world now, with the Kaiser's abdication, and the fall of the Ottoman Empire," Nicholas admitted.

Konstantin, certain that Nicholas was about to outlaw his choice of a bride, felt his heart sink.

"But I agree with your father's position, Kostya," Nicholas continued. "It certainly would have been an equal marriage before the Kaiser's abdication, no question about it. I'm inclined to continue viewing it as such, on the same presumption that the descendants of the former French monarchy, and other monarchies, were of former ruling houses."

Konstantin felt his relief surge through his veins. "Thank you, Your Imperial Majesty," he said.

"When will you ask her?" Nicholas inquired, smiling.

"I haven't decided yet," Konstantin admitted.

"I would be careful as to where you do it," Nicholas advised seriously, his smile disappearing. "Europe is a mess right now, and going to Germany before the Peace Conference could be problematic."

"Would Your Imperial Majesty be amenable to the proposal happening in Paris?" Ioann asked, and Konstantin was grateful for both his presence of mind and his solution.

"I think that's a good idea," Nicholas said. He looked at Konstantin. "You can travel with us to the Peace Conference. Why don't you write to Pilar and ask her to meet us there?"

"I will," Konstantin said. He and Ioann rose, and Konstantin was eager to leave before Nicholas changed his mind.

Nicholas rose also, and Alexei, seeing his father stand, stood up from his chair at the nearby table. "One last thing, Kostya, Ioannchick," Nicholas said. "I'll be meeting with several Balkan delegations later this week. I'd like your regiments to be there with me to greet them when they arrive."

"Absolutely, Your Imperial Majesty," Konstantin said.

Ioann also nodded his assent. "Alexander of Serbia has written to me already, saying that he would be coming. He wants to see Elena and the kids while he's here."

"Of course- Elena is his sister," Nicholas said. "I would have been surprised if you hadn't heard from him."

Ioann waited until he and Konstantin were leaving the Palace to speak again. "Elena also thinks Alexander will take the time here in Russia to propose to Olga," he said.

"So maybe Nicholas will get at least one of the weddings he wants," Konstantin said.

"I hope you get the wedding you want too, Kostya," Ioann said as they were driven back to the Marble Palace. "I haven't forgotten that your last proposal was rejected."

Konstantin clenched his teeth as he looked out the window of the motor car in which they were being driven. *I haven't forgotten either*, he thought. *It better not happen again.*

Two days later, Konstantin stood at attention as the foreign delegations poured into the train station at Tsarskoe Selo. The Order of St. George stood out on his chest, the orange ribbon and sparkling diamonds calling attention to themselves. Konstantin, seeing the decoration out of the corner of his eye as he stared forward, felt his chest swell with pride.

The first delegation to arrive was Alexander of Serbia's, and Alexander exited his train looking every inch a high-ranking royal. *He fought in the War too*, Konstantin thought. His respect for Alexander grew as Nicholas, Alexandra and their family greeted the handsome prince who was acting as Regent for his ill father.

Konstantin smiled as Alexander greeted Ioann and asked after his nieces and nephew. Ioann replied with a large grin on his face. *Ioann's marriage is one reason the Serbians are our allies*, Konstantin thought. *That would only be reinforced if Sandro proposes to Olga.*

Then the Romanian delegation arrived, and the sight of Queen Marie instantly reminded Konstantin of the last time they'd met, seven years earlier. *I haven't forgotten the expression on her face when she told me I wasn't good enough for her daughter.* He took a deep breath and stared straight ahead. *That feels like a long time ago, though,* he realized. *I really feel like a different person than I was when I asked for Elizabeth's hand in marriage. These last four years of war have changed me quite a bit- how could they not? But they also put the rest of my life on hold.*

He thought of Pilar again. *I have to get a move on that. Meeting her in Paris is a good idea. I'll start composing a letter as soon as this event is over.* He watched as Queen Marie's youngest daughter, the nearly ten-year-old Ileana, grinned at Alexei. *Ileana is adorable,* he conceded. *At least some of our family gets along.*

When the Bulgarian delegation arrived, Konstantin watched as Nicholas greeted King Boris and his cabinet. Then he watched as Boris eyed the Grand Duchess Tatiana Nicholaievna, Nicholas' second daughter. She and Olga were smiling widely and talking to Alexander. *Guess I'm not the only one who's thinking of my marriage possibilities,* Konstantin thought. *Nicolas was right- under any other circumstances, Olga and Tatiana would definitely be married by now. The Great War didn't just end a lot of lives, it suspended the lives of everyone who survived.*

It was January, 1919, when the Imperial train steamed out of Tsarskoe Selo, bound for Paris. Konstantin had his own compartment, and he kept to himself as much as possible. *I don't want to get in the way of Nicky's preparation for this conference,* he thought. *And I don't want to distract Alexei too much, either. He needs the political experience- he should stay with Nicky.*

The destruction that Konstantin saw all around him as the train moved forward made him yearn for the beauty of the pre-war years. Everywhere he looked, train tracks had been blown apart and were surrounded by down trees, burnt out lorries and even the bodies of dead horses. *Parts of Russia were destroyed as badly as other parts of Europe,* he thought. *I hope there's the will to rebuild- and to prevent this type of war from ever happening again.*

When the train arrived in Paris, Konstantin was overwhelmed by the crowds awaiting them. Hordes of people stood at the train station and cheered as the Imperial train, with its signature double-headed eagle, pulled into the station. "This is a madhouse," Konstantin said to Nicholas and Alexei.

Nicholas nodded his assent, but Alexei, happy as ever to meet new people, grinned and waved at the people on the platform. Many waved back. Many more took photographs.

Konstantin was only too happy to make it to the quiet of his hotel room, where a telegram awaited him. "Am safely in Paris. Meet by the water at 5 o'clock tomorrow?" it read. Underneath the text was Pilar's neat signature. Konstantin's face split into a grin.

The next day, a few minutes before the appointed hour, Konstantin paced nervously along the banks of the Seine River. It was already nearly dark, and a light fog hung in the air. The gas lamps all around were just beginning to be lit, and one by one, their golden light shone on the water droplets in the air around them. The light was also reflected on the swirling water of the river in front of them.

Then Konstantin caught sight of a familiar figure coming towards him, her umbrella unfurled above her head. *Pilar,* he thought with a grin, and then noticed her mother just behind her. *Of course,* he thought. *Maria wouldn't let her daughter meet me unchaperoned.*

"Hello," Pilar said brightly when she got within earshot of Konstantin.

"Good evening," Konstantin replied, and gave Maria a nod. "How were your travels from Bavaria?"

"As well as could be expected," Maria said. Then she dropped back to allow Konstantin and Pilar to walk along the riverfront side by side. Still, she was never too far behind them.

"So many of the railroads were destroyed in the war," Pilar said.

"Yes, I know," Konstantin said. "As were many of Europe's cities. It's a real shame."

Pilar nodded. "War is such a horror," she said. "I'm glad you've survived unharmed."

"I can't express how grateful I am," Konstantin admitted. "I lost one brother, and one brother-in-law, and yet the devastation could have been even worse." He took a deep breath and looked back at Maria to make sure she was sufficiently behind them on the snow-covered path. When he was satisfied, he looked back at Pilar. "Listen, Pilar, you made an impression on me the first time we met at that church all those years ago. I'm sorry it's taken me such a long time to come around."

Pilar smiled. "I remember the pain you were in the first time we met," she said. "It's not easy to handle that level of rejection, especially in the gossip cauldron of royal Europe."

Konstantin smiled in return. "You have always understood me," he said.

"Well, I was drawn to you too the first time we met. And I've been impressed by your growth and strength since then. Your service during the War was filled with courage."

"I am honored that you think so highly of me." Konstantin felt his stomach clench and his heart rate rise. "And I would be honored if you would marry me."

Pilar stopped and looked at him. For a moment, Konstantin thought she would refuse, and he was certain that his world was going to fall out under him. But then Pilar smiled. "Absolutely," she said. "I would be happy to."

Simultaneously, they both turned and looked back at Maria, but she had stopped some distance behind them and was looking over the railing into the Seine. Konstantin and Pilar faced forward again and continued walking. Konstantin reached out and took Pilar's hand. Pilar squeezed his hand in return. Then they looked at each other and smiled. Konstantin felt his heart swell.

Hand in hand, they walked along the river, breathing in the scents of snow and happiness.

## THE FAMILY GATHERS

Prince Konstantin Konstantinovich of Russia took a deep breath as he sat down next to Princess Pilar of Bavaria. Her parents, Ludwig and Maria, sat on her other side. *Ludwig doesn't like me, I know it,* he thought. *I think he's glad that Pilar is finally engaged, but I heard he wished it was to a more senior royal.*

But Ludwig's expression was pleasant as he looked around the room, watching the couples dancing and the musicians playing. "This whole ceremony has really been beautiful," he said.

"This is my first time in Belgrade," Pilar added.

Konstantin nodded. "Olga Nicholaievna is happy to finally be getting married, and I think she and Alexander will be happy together."

"I wondered when he would finally settle down," Ludwig said. "He's going to be king one day, so he's certainly a good match."

Konstantin had to struggle to keep his expression neutral. His kept his hands in his lap, where they remained hidden by the long tablecloth on the table in front of him. Then he felt Pilar take his hand, and he smiled at her, grateful for both the gesture and the fact that it, too, was hidden by the tablecloth. Then he took another deep breath and smelled the flowers that were at the center of the table.

Konstantin looked around the room, searching for the bride and groom. When he saw them, he smiled. Olga's long wedding dress trailed across the floor as she spoke to her brother Alexei, the heir to the Russian throne. Alexei then looked at his new brother-and-law and smiled as he spoke. *Good for him,* Konstantin thought of Alexei. *He could have inherited his parents' shy natures, but he hasn't. Besides, after four sisters, Alyosha could use another male figure besides Nicholas, especially one that will inherit a throne like he will.*

Out of the corner of his eye, Konstantin saw the chair next to him being pulled away from the table. He looked up to see his younger brother Igor sitting down next to him. "Olga seems really happy," Igor said. "Alexander too."

Konstantin nodded. "So is Nicholas," he said, glancing over to the next table, where the Russian Tsar sat watching his oldest daughter with a smile. "He really likes Alexander. He was hoping for awhile that Alexander would propose to one of his daughters."

"Well, Alexander studied in Russia for a long time. It makes sense in a lot of ways." Igor looked around the room. "The wedding has been really nice," he added. "Very colorful. Serbian national costumes are fabulous."

Konstantin and Pilar both nodded in agreement.

"It looks like you two will be next," Igor continued, looking back at his brother and future sister-in-law. "It's April already, so your wedding is only two months away."

"I'm looking forward to it," Konstantin said with a smile.

"Are all your preparations complete?" Igor asked.

"Almost," Pilar said. "We don't have too much more to plan."

Just then, the Grand Duchess Anastasia, Olga's youngest sister, sat on Igor's other side and placed a plate of Russian gingerbread thumbprint cookies in front of him.

"Ooh, gingerbread thumbprint cookies," Igor said as he and Anastasia both took one. "These are my favorite." He held out the plate to Konstantin and Pilar, who took a cookie each before passing the plate down to Maria and Ludwig. Igor looked back at Anastasia. "Where did you get those?" he asked.

"I snuck into the kitchen," Anastasia said, tossing her long curls over her shoulder.

"What?" Ludwig asked, unsure if he'd heard Anastasia correctly.

Igor and Konstantin were already laughing, though, and Pilar was smiling too. "Relax, Papa," she said.

Just then, Alexei swung by the table. "Are those gingerbread thumbprint cookies?" he asked.

Anastasia rolled her eyes at her brother. "Can't hide anything from you," she said.

"Not if it's sweet," Alexei agreed as he grabbed a couple of cookies.

"Can I have the plate back, Alyosha?" Igor asked.

Alexei dumped the cookies into a bowl on the table and handed Igor the empty plate. Anastasia and Konstantin burst into laughter, and Pilar joined them. Even Ludwig and Maria were having trouble suppressing smiles.

"Oh, you-" Igor began. Then he thought better of finishing his sentence that way. "The cookies too, please, Alyosha," he said instead.

Alexei laughed and handed the bowl of cookies to his cousin. Igor made a face at him as Alexei turned and walked to the next table, where his parents sat. His mother, the Empress Alexandra, continued watching Anastasia. *Uh oh,* Konstantin thought, noticing Alexandra's pointed stare before she looked away.

"Uh oh," Igor said, biting his lip.

"What?" Anastasia asked.

"You mother was keeping an eye on us."

"She's worried I'll eat all the cookies," Anastasia said, reaching for another.

"She needn't worry about you," Igor replied, taking two.

"She'd be better off keeping an eye on Tanya," Konstantin agreed, mentioning Anastasia's older sister.

"Why?" Anastasia asked, looking around. "Where is Tanya, anyway?"

"Exactly my point," Konstantin said. "She just slipped out of the room with Boris of Bulgaria following her."

"She probably has to go to the toilet," Anastasia said. "Hopefully he won't follow her in there."

"I think Bo's interested in marrying Tanya," Konstantin said. *I've thought that for awhile now.*

"Me too," Anastasia said. "I thought he would have proposed already, but I guess he didn't want to overshadow Olga's big day."

Igor glanced back at the door behind them, then at Anastasia, then at Alexandra, who was eying them again.

Konstantin followed Igor's gaze, and saw Alexandra look away. *I'll bet Alexandra is expecting Boris to propose too,* he thought. *And I'm sure she's also thinking of matches for Anastasia.* He took a deep breath. *I'm so glad I already have my match and I don't have to think about that anymore.* He looked over at Pilar. "Would you care to dance?" he asked as the musicians struck up a new song.

"Absolutely," she said. "I'd love to."

# CONTINUED ENDINGS

It was the night before Konstantin's wedding, and Konstantin felt as though he were swimming in a sea of calm happiness. Still, as he walked through the halls of Pavlovsk, he could not shake a slight feeling of uneasiness. *It's not about the wedding,* he realized. *It's that I can't find Tatiana.*

Konstantin had just spent several hours with the rest of his siblings and their mother, playing billiards with his brothers and interrupting the game occasionally to dance with Vera, his youngest sister, still only fourteen years old. It had taken many rounds of laughter and billiards for Konstantin to realize that it had gotten to be nearly midnight.

"How did it get to be so late so fast?" Konstantin asked.

"It's because you're happy," his oldest brother, Ioann, said. "Now get some sleep. Tomorrow is going to be a long day."

So, Konstantin said goodnight to his family and started down the Palace's long hallways to his apartments. That was when he realized that Tatiana had been missing from the family's festivities. *Where could she be?* he wondered, and headed for Tatiana's rooms in the Palace.

The rooms were mostly dark when Konstantin arrived. Only the moonlight, coming in through the open window, provided any illumination. The whole scene convinced Konstantin that his sister was somewhere else- until he caught sight of her lying on the couch. "Tanya, are you awake?" he whispered.

Tatiana turned her head, and even in the semi-darkness, Konstantin could see the blue of her eyes, a light, nearly translucent shade that mirrored his own eyes. For the first time, he could also see the tears that ran down her face.

"Tanya, what's wrong?" Konstantin asked, turning on a lamp and going over to his sister.

Tatiana sat up and looked at Konstantin as he sat next to her on the couch. "I miss my husband, that's all," he said.

Konstantin wasn't surprised to hear her response. He, too, missed the brother-in-law that shared his name, and who had been killed in action during the first few months of the Great War. "Kostya's death was a tragedy, both for Russia and for you," he agreed.

"I so longed for that marriage, and I was so happy when it finally happened," Tatiana said.

"I remember," Konstantin replied. "Did you know that it was your happiness, and Ioann's happiness with Elena, that made me want to get married myself?"

Tatiana looked at her brother and wiped the tears from her face, even as more kept flowing. "And now our situations have been reversed," she said. "You're just embarking on your matrimonial journey, and I'm a widow with two young children."

"Come on Tanya," Konstantin said, handing his sister a handkerchief. "You can't think like that. You have a long future ahead of you."

Tatiana shrugged. "A future for what?" she asked. "I am nothing without Kostya."

"That's not true at all," Konstantin replied. "You have so much to give. You could do anything." He took a deep breath. "It's been a few years since Kostya's death, and your children are growing up. Might you consider remarrying?"

"A widow with two young children?" Tatiana repeated. "I doubt anyone will have me."

"I don't think that's true either," Konstantin said. "Give yourself a chance."

"I've thought of becoming a nun, too," Tatiana said.

"Retreating from life?" Konstantin asked. "I'd rather see you out in society, visible as a member of the Imperial family."

"And yet becoming a nun after the death of a spouse is not unheard of in our family. Aunt Ella did it."

"I know that," Konstantin said. "But she was much older than you when she founded her convent." He looked at his sister and sighed. Her sadness still remained, both on her face and hanging over her head. "I hate to see you like this," Konstantin added.

Tatiana shrugged and looked away. Konstantin continued looking at her, his heart breaking in the face of her unhappiness- unhappiness that contrasted to his own mood and desperate longing for the next day and all its blessings. At the same time, Konstantin realized that he was out of words. *I genuinely don't know how to comfort her anymore,* he thought.

At that moment, Vera appeared in the doorway, looking concerned. "I thought I told you to go to bed," Konstantin told her, even if he was relieved that she was there.

"So what if you did?" Vera teased her brother. "I wanted to check on Tanya."

Behind her, their mother, the Grand Duchess Elizaveta Mavrikievna, appeared, and Konstantin could see his four brothers crowding the hallway behind their mother. Konstantin took a deep breath and looked back at Tatiana. *I'd hate to have the whole family see Tanya's pain,* he thought. *But maybe they can help her more than I can.*

"I'm fine, I'm fine," Tatiana said as she stood up. She had wiped the tears from her face, and her eyes looked clearer.

"Good," Elizaveta told her daughter. "I'd hate to see you crying on the eve of such a happy event."

"I'm not crying," Tatiana said.

*Not anymore*, Konstantin thought.

"Where are my children?" Tatiana asked.

"Asleep in the nursery, where they should be," Elizaveta replied.

Konstantin's brothers all pushed past their mother and into the room. "You should go to sleep, Kostya," Ioann advised his younger brother, as his wife Elena, standing behind him, nodded. "Tomorrow is going to be a long day for you."

"It'll be a long day for all of us," Elizaveta said, shooing her children out into the hall. "We should all get some rest."

Konstantin looked back at Tatiana. "I'm fine now," she said. "I'll see you tomorrow."

Konstantin's face broke into a grin. "See you tomorrow."

# A HAPPY FUTURE

Konstantin drew himself up straight, feeling the confines of his military uniform as he stiffened his spine. He closed his eyes and took a deep breath, willing his heart to slow down and his anxiety to evacuate his body. When he opened his eyes, he was still in the small room directly adjacent to the chapel of the Winter Palace. He was also alone, and glad for the solitude.

*I love this place,* he thought as he eyed the golden parquet floor, glowing in the morning sunlight. *I love the other palaces too, including the Marble Palace and Pavlovsk. I love St. Petersburg, and I want to live here for the rest of my life.* Konstantin took another deep breath as he pictured St. Isaac's Cathedral, with its green columns and towering iconostasis. He continued picturing the other churches throughout the city, and all of the private chapels in his favorite palaces. Konstantin felt a deep love, like a tight ache in his chest. *I love the whole of this city,* he thought. *I'm so glad to be a Russian, and that my Princess has agreed to come live here and become Russian too.*

He closed his eyes once more and took a slow, deep breath. When he opened his eyes again, the door in front of him, the one leading further into the Palace, slowly opened. For a moment, Konstantin saw nobody in the doorway, and he was certain that the door had opened on its own. Then Princess Pilar of Bavaria stuck her head into the room. Her head was covered by her white wedding veil, which she'd lifted from her face and hung down her back. She grinned broadly when she saw Konstantin.

"What are you doing here?" Konstantin hissed, reaching the door from the middle of the room in two long strides. "We're not supposed to see each other before the ceremony!"

"I know," Pilar said in the same hushed voice. "But I couldn't help myself."

"You're supposed to be upstairs! What did you tell our mothers about where you were going?"

"I said I was going to the toilet."

Konstantin heard a step in the hall behind him. He quickly twisted his head around. Luckily, the room was still empty. He threw his head back towards Pilar. "Someone's coming!" he hissed. "You'd better get back upstairs before anyone sees you!"

Pilar turned around and dashed back up the hallway.

"Take the back passageway!" Konstantin whispered loudly at her retreating form. He closed the door behind her and doubled over into silent laughter. He had barely composed himself when the door across the room opened, and Tsar Nicholas II entered. Tsarevich Alexei, now noticeably taller than his father, was on Nicholas' heels, and he looked excited and happy.

"I'm glad to see you smiling again, finally," Nicholas said to Konstantin as he and Alexei crossed the room.

Konstantin nodded. "I'm glad for it, too," he said. He eyed both Nicholas and Alexei. Nicholas looked old and tired, even with the kind smile on his face. *Four years of a horrendous world war will do that to anyone, even if it's been almost a year since the Great War ended,* Konstantin thought. Even so, he rejoiced internally at how good Alexei looked. *Alyosha's been healthy for awhile now, thanks be to God. He comes of age soon too- I never knew whether I'd see that happen.*

Nicholas continued to smile. "I know your father had wanted to live long enough to give you and each of your siblings a blessing on your wedding day," he said.

Konstantin sighed, and his smile disappeared. "My father is never far from my memory," he said. "Neither is Oleg."

"I think you've become a fine young man, Kostya, worthy of their memories," Nicholas replied.

"Thank you," Konstantin said sincerely.

"Are you ready for the ceremony?" Alexei asked.

"I am," Konstantin replied.

Inside the chapel a short while later, Konstantin smiled broadly as Pilar made her way down the aisle, her long white dress flowing and pearls at her hair. *She looks so beautiful,* he thought. *Even if I knew that already.* Under his smile, he had to clench his teeth so as not to double over with laughter again at the memory of her fleeing down the hallway.

The ceremony began as the priests intoned the Russian Orthodox blessings. Soon, the smell of incense filled the air. Konstantin's four brothers- Ioann, Gavril, Igor and George- took turns holding the nuptial crowns over Konstantin and Pilar's heads. The sunlight streaming in from the window atop the chapel made the gold crowns sparkle.

After several rounds of prayers and singing, the priest picked up two gold wedding bands and made the sign of the cross over Konstantin and Pilar. When the attendant prayers had been repeated three times, the priest placed Pilar's ring in Konstantin's right hand, and placed Konstantin's ring in Pilar's right hand. Slowly, Konstantin placed the ring on the third finger of Pilar's left hand, and she placed his ring on his finger. Then they both grinned at each other.

*Finally,* Konstantin thought, as the priest continued with the service. *This has really been a long time in the making. I am so happy.*

When the long service ended, Konstantin and Pilar were given a few minutes to themselves before the celebratory banquet began. Only a few seconds of their solitude passed before the door to the room opened and Ioann and Gavril snuck in, ducking their heads under the doorway.

"We're supposed to be alone," Konstantin told them, but the grins on his brothers' faces made him smile too.

"I know that," Ioann said as Igor and George snuck into the room as well. "But I just wanted to congratulate you."

"That's what the banquet is for," Konstantin teased.

"So what if it is?" Igor said, holding his arms open to his brother and new sister-in-law.

After a round of hugs, Igor and George went back out the door. Ioann and Gavril followed, remembering only just in time to duck so as not to hit their heads on the top of the doorway. Pilar shook her head as she watched them close the door behind them. "I hope our sons aren't as tall and thin as your brothers are," she teased. "That would be awful."

"It would only be worse if our daughters looked like that," Konstantin said, in the same spirit.

"My God, that would be worse," Pilar agreed. "We could never marry them off. What would we do with them?"

"There's always the circus," Konstantin replied. He and Pilar looked at each other and doubled over laughing.

"It won't come to that," Pilar said when they could breathe again.

"Only because our daughters will be beautiful- and a normal height." Konstantin took both of his bride's hands in his own, feeling the cool wedding ring around her finger. "I am so happy you have finally joined me in matrimony," he said. "I know you weren't eager to leave Bavaria."

"I wasn't," Pilar admitted. "But I left for the best possible reason."

The door to the room opened again, and Konstantin feared another of his brothers' intrusions. Instead, it was the women of the family- his mother and sisters, and Pilar's mother.

Elizaveta Mavrikievna smiled at her son. "Are you ready for the banquet?" she asked.

"I am," Konstantin replied. He looked at Pilar. "Shall we go inside?"

"Yes," she replied. "Let's go celebrate."

# AN INCREASE OF WEALTH

Three months after their marriage, Prince Konstantin and Princess Pilar walked through the countryside outside of Moscow. Konstantin inhaled deeply, breathing in the smell of leaves that were changing from their green summer lushness to their colorful fall counterparts.

Next to him, Pilar looked around at the foliage and smiled. "This is beautiful," she said. "I never would have guessed that such beautiful open space existed so closely outside the city."

Konstantin nodded. "I always envied Uncle Sergei and Aunt Ella's estate at Ilinskoe. It's just outside Moscow too, and a total paradise."

"Does Ella still own the place?" Pilar asked, picturing the beautiful woman who had become a nun after Sergei's violent murder.

Konstantin shook his head. "It belongs to their nephew Dmitri now, but he's been in exile in Persia for the last three years. The estate is barely used."

"Have you contacted Dmitri recently? Perhaps he'd let us stay there in his absence."

"Perhaps."

"Perhaps we could offer to help with the upkeep, if we're there often enough," Pilar suggested, trying to get a sense of what her husband was thinking.

"We could also get our own country estate in this area," Konstantin said. "I'd love to stay at Ilinskoe occasionally, but it's too large for me to want to offer to buy it from Dmitri."

"Our own country estate," Pilar said. "I like that idea." All of a sudden, though, her pleasant expression changed to a grimace.

"Are you alright?" Konstantin asked.

Pilar took a deep breath and nodded, but her expression did not change. "I've been feeling this way on and off for the last week or two," she said.

"What way?" Konstantin pressed, feeling increasingly worried. *I don't like her expression at all.*

"Slightly sick to my stomach."

"Must be the change to Russian food."

Pilar shook her head, but at least she now looked amused. "I've been eating Russian food since we got engaged, and it's never disagreed with me before."

"What, then?" Konstantin was starting to feel slightly chilled, and he wondered whether the autumn air was responsible.

Pilar contemplated the question. "Why don't you call the doctor?" she said finally.

Konstantin was unhappy with that answer, and his face showed it.


Two days later, Konstantin stood watching as Dr. Ivanov, his personal physician, examined Pilar. "What do you think?" Konstantin asked after a few minutes, unable to take the doctor's silence any longer.

"I think she's probably with child," Ivanov replied.

Konstantin's eyebrows shot up. Pilar did not look surprised. "You knew," Konstantin said to her.

"I suspected," Pilar admitted. "I missed my monthly curse, and I haven't been feeling well."

They spent the next nine months watching Pilar's belly grow. Konstantin delighted in the baby's development, especially when he could feel the child kicking against Pilar's stomach. "I'm really looking forward to having this child," he said one evening as his hand made its way around her stomach, searching for the next spot where the baby's foot might hit.

One morning in June, when the golden sunlight bathed the palace and everything around it, Pilar began groaning with labor pains. Konstantin called Dr. Ivanov, and then, at the doctor's orders, retreated into his study to await the outcome. Once he was alone, he felt his nervousness slither up his throat like a snake, threatening to choke him. *We're having our first child at twenty-nine years old,* he thought. *I hope that doesn't adversely affect the outcome.*

For a few minutes, Konstantin stood at the window, staring up at a sky that was still a deep blue. *Maybe I should call Ioann or Tanya,* he thought. *They've already had children. Perhaps they can reassure me.* Then he shook his head at himself. *Ioann has four children to look after, and Elena is pregnant with their fifth. I don't want to disturb them.*

So, Konstantin busied himself with matters of his regiment- uniforms, training, and whatever else he could find to fill the time. It was shortly after 11 o'clock at night, in the midst of St. Petersburg's magical white nights where the sun barely touches the horizon, when Dr. Ivanov appeared in his study. Konstantin looked at him.

"You have a healthy son," the doctor said.

Konstantin leapt to his feet, pushed past the doctor, and dashed upstairs to find Pilar. Dr. Ivanov followed him, and when they entered the room, Pilar was still surrounded by Ivanov's assistants and the midwife. Konstantin stood in the doorway as if nailed to the floor, looking at his wife with round eyes. "How are you?" he asked.

"Tired," she said.

Konstantin heard a baby wail, and finally, his feet began functioning enough to carry him over to his wife's bedside, where she held a swaddled infant. Konstantin pulled up a chair and sat next to her, leaning in to see their new child. Pilar held up the infant so that Konstantin could see him, and then handed him their son. For a few minutes, Konstantin sat spellbound, looking at the little person in his arms. "Hello," he finally whispered.

Then he noticed that the doctor, assistants, and midwife had all crept out of the room, leaving him and Pilar alone with the baby. *I didn't even hear them go,* he thought. He looked at Pilar and smiled. She smiled back. Then he looked back at the baby.

*I can't believe my parents did this nine times,* he thought, and cursed himself when the words came out of his mouth.

"We're definitely not having that many," Pilar said.

"Definitely not," Konstantin agreed. *We started too late, and nine is too many.* "I would like at least a few more, though."

"How about you enjoy this one before we start discussing more?" Pilar asked, scrunching up her face at her husband.

"I am enjoying this one," Konstantin said, his face breaking out into a grin. He stood up, still holding the baby, and began exaggeratedly marching around the room, throwing his legs out stiffly at the waist as he sang to the child.

"You are ridiculous," Pilar said.

"I know," Konstantin, still grinning. He sat back down in the chair next to the bed. "We have to name him."

"Do you still want to use Oleg, after your brother?"

A lump formed in Konstantin's throat as he thought of his talented younger brother, killed only a few months into the fighting of the Great War. "It's too soon," he said. *Even if it has been nearly six years since Oleg perished. Maybe it will always be too soon.*

"What about Sergei?" Pilar said, referring to another name that had been on their list. "I like that one- it means 'protector.'"

Konstantin nodded. "I like it too," he said. "And it isn't one of those names that our family has used to death." He looked down at his tiny son, who was now staring back him with wide eyes as he began to wriggle around in his arms. "Hello Sergei," he said. "I've been waiting a long time to meet you."

# DEATH OF A TSAR

It was late August in St. Petersburg. Sunlight streamed through the windows of the palace Strelna, where Prince Konstantin Konstantinovich was eating breakfast with his family. Holding a teacup in one hand, Konstantin sighed with happiness as he watched his wife Pilar cradle two-month-old Sergei as she finished eating. Konstantin eyed Sergei, who, despite his young age, seemed fascinated by the toy plane sitting on the table in front of him. Then Sergei reached for his mother to start nursing again.

"He certainly has a healthy appetite," Pilar said.

"Yes, he does," Konstantin replied, keeping his eyes on his son, whose nearly translucent blond hair was finally getting longer. "And he loves those planes, more so than the rest of his toys."

Pilar eyed her husband with amusement. "Don't think I didn't notice that all of your brothers gave him military toys," she said. "Gavril gave him guns, Igor a train set, Ioann these planes, George a number of toy soldiers."

"We Romanov men are all about the military," Konstantin replied. "We're just training him." He smiled as he looked back at Sergei. "Besides, Ioann got these planes custom made from the actual plane factory that he toured with Nicholas and Alexei."

Konstantin was about to say something else when the bells of the nearby cathedrals suddenly started ringing, all at once. The mournful cacophony made Konstantin and Pilar jump. They looked at each other quizzically, and Konstantin, his brow furrowed in confusion, put his cloth napkin on the table and pushed his seat back. Hauling himself to his feet, he went to the window and looked outside. All around, the bells continued tolling. *What's going on?* Konstantin wondered.

Suddenly, the telephone jangled, making Konstantin jump again. He frowned even further as he reached for the phone. "Hello?"

"Kostya, it's Alexei," the young heir to the Romanov throne said on the other end.

"Alyosha, what's happening?" Konstantin asked. "The cathedral bells here suddenly all started ringing. Is something going on?"

"Yes, my father bids you live long," Alexei replied, and his voice sounded both rough and uncertain.

"Damn it," Konstantin cursed. He instantly regretted the harsh words, but they were out before he could stop them. *We were just celebrating Alyosha's sixteenth birthday and coming of age three days ago. Those celebrations were splendid. This will be a change altogether.* "I'm sorry," he said. "When did it happen?"

"Overnight," Alexei replied.

"Is there anything I can do?"

"Not right now. I have to finish calling the family first."

"Alright. Let me know if I can help with anything." Konstantin hung up the phone and stared out the window, his emotions churning. *Alyosha just turned sixteen,* he thought. *That's the youngest age a Tsar is allowed to rule on his own by law, without a regent. But Alyosha seems so young- can he do this on his own?*

"Kostya, what happened?" Pilar asked from behind him.

Konstantin turned from the window. Feeling as though his mind were separated from the rest of his body, Konstantin felt his whole body turn on a single pivot, as if a steel rod ran through him, from his skull to the floor. "That was Alexei," he said. "Nicholas is dead."

"Oh, my God," Pilar said, standing up and maneuvering Sergei onto her shoulder. "Does that mean that Alexei is tsar now?"

"Yes." Konstantin still felt as though his words were emanating from someone else. His eyes went to his wife's face. "He's just a child, Pilar."

Pilar bit her lip.

"I have to get over to the Winter Palace." Finally, Konstantin started moving again, towards the door of the room.

"Wait," Pilar said. "I'll come with you. We can leave Sergei with his nurses."

At that moment, the phone rang again, and Konstantin picked it up. "Hello?"

"Kostya, it's Igor," his younger brother said. He sounded tense. "Did you hear from Alyosha?"

"Yes."

"I'm heading over to the Palace. I was supposed to be on duty anyway as Nicky's Aide-De-Camp. Do you want come?"

"Yes."

A few minutes later, Sergei was safely in his nursery and Igor was driving up outside Strelna. "I can't believe this, Kostya," Igor said as they sped to the Winter Palace. "Alyosha just turned sixteen. Is he going to be able to rule an entire empire on his own?"

"He won't be on his own," Konstantin said adamantly. "There may need to be a regency of some sort- maybe Uncle Misha. At the very least, all of us are here to help him."

Konstantin felt somewhat reassured in these sentiments when they arrived at the Winter Palace to find Ioann arriving with Elena. "Gavril's here already, and Mama's on her way with Tatiana, George and Vera," Ioann said as they all went inside.

Inside the Winter Palace, they found Gavril comforting Alexei in one of the drawing rooms, even as his own tears flowed down his face. *Gavril served as Nicky's ADC for a good while*, Konstantin thought as he hugged Alexei. *He was close to Nicky too.* He eyed Alexei as his wife and brothers hugged their young cousin. *What is he thinking?* Konstantin wondered.

Alexei sighed as he sat down in one of the room's armchairs. "I've heard that Papa felt unprepared to be Tsar when his father passed away," he said with a sigh. "Now I know the feeling."

Konstantin nodded. The story of Nicholas breaking down and sobbing upon his father's death, wondering how he would rule the empire, was well known in the family. *He couldn't even pull himself together to notify the rest of the family of Alexander's death*, Konstantin thought. *Another of our cousins had to do it.*

Konstantin knew his brothers were thinking the same thing when Ioann said, "well, Alyosha, at least you had the wherewithal to notify the family yourself."

"Barely," Alexei said. "I feel like I've just been acting automatically, without any feeling." Then, all of a sudden, he doubled over and started sobbing.

Konstantin, Pilar, Ioann, Elena, and Gavril surrounded him, draping their arms around him and rubbing his back. "You're not alone- you have all of us as a resource," Konstantin said. "Don't be afraid to call us if you need to."

"Thanks," Alexei said. The word sounded strangled through his tears.

Just then, Konstantin's mother, the Grand Duchess Elizaveta Mavrikievna, came in with his brother George. Both of them hugged Alexei. "Where are Vera and Tatiana?" Konstantin whispered to George as their mother spoke to Alexei.

"In the next room with Anastasia, Marie and Igor," George whispered back.

Konstantin glanced around the room. *I didn't even notice that Igor slipped out,* he thought. He went into the next room, where Igor sat next to Anastasia, and Vera and Tatiana surrounded Marie and Anastasia. Slowly, the Palace filled up with the large extended Imperial family. That night, as darkness slowly descended on St. Petersburg, the first requiem mass for the departed Tsar was held.

The funeral services were held nearly a week later, after Nicholas' body had lay in state. As Konstantin walked on foot behind the casket, he eyed Alexei's tall frame up ahead of him. *He's significantly taller than Nicholas was, and he carries himself with more authority,* Konstantin thought. *But we haven't had a sixteen-year-old Tsar since the 1600s. Things have changed since then.*

Konstantin looked around at the people surrounding the route that the funeral procession was taking. Thousands upon thousands of people had lined the route to pay their respects, and Konstantin could see many of those people eyeing Alexei. *They're also wondering what kind of Tsar he'll be,* Konstantin thought.

In the Cathedral of the Fortress of St. Peter and Paul, the priests chanted the funeral liturgy and lit incense. Konstantin felt his nose get clogged by the incense, and felt his eyes clogged by tears. Next to him, Pilar held his hand, and Konstantin felt reassured by her presence. At the same time, Konstantin's eyes found Alexei again. *Please, God, help him through this difficult time,* Konstantin prayed. *Give him the strength to be a firm but compassionate ruler. Allow him to correct the mistakes of Nicholas' reign- don't keep him cloistered in the Palace, sequestered away from the people over whom he reigns.*

After the funeral, Konstantin and his family gathered back at Pavlovsk, the palace in which he'd grown up, and Konstantin was glad for the familiar surroundings. One morning in particular, he held Sergei and stood at the window, noticing the color that was beginning to seep into the trees around the Palace, and the fact that some leaves were already falling. *A change in reign, a change in seasons,* he thought.

Several days later, the phone at Pavlovsk rang, and when Gavril answered it, he smiled. "Are you back at work already, Alyosha?" he asked.

Both Konstantin and Igor eyed Gavril, wondering what Alexei needed from them. Ioann also appeared in the doorway to listen to the conversation.

Gavril listened to the young tsar, and then teased him, "just put in the same number of hours your father worked, and you'll be fine." On the other end, Alexei replied, and Gavril laughed. Then he said, "I'm sure he is, but let me put him on." He handed the phone to Igor. "It's Alyosha," he said. "He's got your petition to be his ADC rather than Nicholas'."

Igor took the phone and listened to what Alexei had to say. "Yes, I'm still interested," he said. "I can start as soon as I finish some loose ends with my regiment." He listened for a minute before asking, "what do you need a pistol for, Alyosha? Are you upset with me already?" Then he said, "are you sure that's a good idea?" Then, "alright, I'll get the pistol."

Konstantin bit his lip as he listened to the conversation and watched Igor hang up when it was over. "What was that about?" he asked. "What is Alyosha arming himself against?"

"He has a meeting with Vladimir Ilyich Lenin," Igor replied. "He wants to be prepared."

"Lenin, the revolutionary?" Ioann asked, coming into the room. "I don't like that at all."

"Me neither," Konstantin said.

"I don't think it's a great idea either," Igor admitted. "But at least Alyosha seems to be approaching it cautiously."

"But you're going to be his ADC now, right?" Gavril asked Igor.

Igor nodded.

"Take care of him, Igor," Konstantin said.

"I will," Igor promised.

"I mean it, Igor," Konstantin said, putting his hands on Igor's shoulders and practically shaking him. "This is a sixteen-year-old kid who just inherited a three hundred year old empire."

"I know that," Igor said, pushing Konstantin's hands away. "No one wants to see him succeed as much as I do. I will protect him with my life."

# GAME TIME

Konstantin grinned as Igor was led into the game room of his Palace at Strelna, in the suburbs of St. Petersburg. "I'm glad you made it over safely," he said as he placed a set of billiard balls on the billiard table. A fire roared behind him and the Palace's electric lights gleamed off the balls. Outside in the December evening, heavily falling snow added to the white carpet that blanketed the grounds of the Palace.

Igor's grin made his round cheeks crinkle. "I'm glad I could come," he said. "This is one of the few nights I haven't been working. I think I've ended up sleeping at the Winter Palace or at Tsarskoe Selo more than at my own apartments."

"At least Alyosha is making you work," Konstantin teased. "That's a change."

"Shut up," Igor replied, but he was smiling as he leaned over, stick in hand, to send the billiard balls flying across the table.

"Hey," Konstantin said, swinging his stick and lightly whacking Igor on the arm. "Who said you could take the first shot?"

Igor straightened up and watched with mock indignation as the billiard balls began rolling across the table. "You ruined my shot!"

"That's because I didn't give you permission to start playing just yet."

Igor swung his stick at his older brother, and Konstantin blocked it by holding his stick out like a sword. In a second, both brothers were swinging at each other with increasing speed. Then Igor's stick missed Konstantin's, and poked Konstantin in the shoulder- hard. "Ouch!" Konstantin yelped.

"Boys, boys, boys," someone said from the doorway, and Konstantin and Igor looked up to see Pilar, holding little Sergei.

Konstantin and Igor stood up straight and looked at each other. Then they burst out laughing. Pilar joined them, and even little Sergei's face lit up with a grin.

"Awww, Gega," Konstantin said. He put down his billiard stick and went to take his son from Pilar's arms. In a second, he was snuggling Sergei against his chest.

Igor continued smiling as he eyed Pilar's swollen belly. "When are you expecting your next one?"

"In March," Pilar said. "Sergei won't be quite three years old yet, but I think it's alright."

"Ioann was almost wondering if he and Elena would have another," Konstantin said. "If they do, our new one will have a cousin his age."

"I can't believe he'd think of having another one," Igor said. "He's got five already."

"We'll see what happens," Konstantin said. "He and Elena only had Vyacheslav because, after one boy and three girls, Ioann wanted another son."

"Well, if his sixth one turns out to be a boy, at least they'll have three of each," Igor said.

Konstantin nodded. "Ioann would be very happy with that symmetry."

Pilar held out her hands for Sergei. "Why don't you finish your billiards game?" she said.

"Because we'd have to start it in order to finish it," Konstantin said. He and Igor laughed. Then Konstantin handed Sergei back to Pilar and picked up his billiard stick.

Igor rearranged the balls on the table as Pilar, cradling Sergei, took a seat next to the fire.

Konstantin smiled at his wife. Then a feeling of peace spread over him as he watched Igor neatly line up the billiard balls. *This is so nice,* he thought. *The Great War has been over for three years, the country is at peace, it's almost Christmas, and I have the wife and son I want with another child on the way.*

"Do you want the first shot?" Igor asked as he finished rearranging the billiard balls and stood up straight.

"Sure," Konstantin replied. He bent over, and aimed his stick at the ball closest to him. Then, with a quick motion, he thrust his stick across the table. It hit the first ball with a loud "thwack," sending the rest of the balls spinning across the table.

When the balls had stopped moving, Igor leaned over and took a shot. The brothers played together in silence for awhile before Konstantin asked after their young Tsar. *I've been worried about Alyosha's health since he took that fall in the Crimea,* he thought. "How is Alyosha feeling?" he said. "Is he still walking with crutches?"

Igor nodded. "He still has them, but he doesn't really need them," he said. "He's much better now. He was angry with himself that his vacation ended with him getting injured that way, but that was a year ago. I think he's gotten over it."

"What's the matter with him, Igor?" Konstantin asked. "Nicholas and Alexandra spent all of their energy making sure his condition was a state secret."

Igor nodded. "I know," he said. "He's clearly been ill his whole life and I never had any idea with what. Did you know I asked him what his problem was when I first started working as his Aide-de-Camp?"

"You asked him directly?" Konstantin said, his eyebrows raised. "I'm impressed. What did he say?"

"That he has hemophilia."

Konstantin gasped. "The hereditary blood disease?"

Igor nodded. "Alyosha also said he's tired of keeping it a secret. He may end up making it public somehow."

"That's brave," Konstantin said.

"And a huge change over how he was raised," Igor said, leaning over the billiard table again.

"Alyosha always had a mind of his own," Konstantin said, feeling the heat from the fire on his back as he watched Igor take another shot at the billiards. "Maybe he'll be a stronger ruler than Nicholas was. The dynasty could certainly use the change."

"Russia has always veered towards strong rulers," Igor agreed. "Ivan the terrible, Peter the Great, Catherine the Great. Alexanders II and III were strong also."

"Even so, Alyosha certainly could go the other way, and just be a spoiled brat, except now with a lot of power," Konstantin said. "He was definitely spoiled growing up."

"Probably because of the hemophilia," Igor said.

"It's not really such a surprise that he would have the disease," Pilar interjected from behind them.

"What do you mean?" Konstantin asked his wife.

"Hemophilia runs in royal families of Europe, especially in Germany," Pilar said. "Alexandra's brother died from it."

"Alyosha said that Alexandra feels as though it's her fault he has the disease," Igor said.

"It does pass through the mother," Pilar said. "I can imagine how guilty she must feel. I mean, think about it- she had four daughters when having a son was the only thing that mattered, and when she finally had a son, he could have been killed at any time."

"How do you know so much about hemophilia?" Konstantin asked his wife, turning to look at her.

"Like I said, it runs in the German royal families, especially the ones that were related to Queen Victoria. It was always a factor in our marriage prospects."

Konstantin shook his head as he leaned over the billiard table and took aim at a blue ball. "I'm sure it must be on Alyosha's mind for finding a wife too," he said.

"It wouldn't surprise me," Igor agreed.

"Has he spoken of marriage at all?" Konstantin asked.

Igor shook his head. "No. But he is only seventeen."

"Still, he is Tsar now, and he needs an heir, now more than ever. If he has a disease that could kill him at any time, he should start planning his wedding sooner rather than later."

"I'm sure he's thinking about it," Igor replied.

"And what about you, Igor?" Pilar asked. "Have you given much thought to your own marriage prospects?"

Igor just shrugged, but Konstantin saw a furtive look in his brother's eyes. *He's been thinking about it,* Konstantin realized. "Talk to me, Igor," he said. "Who are you thinking of?"

"Who said I had anyone in mind?" Igor replied.

"Brotherly intuition."

"Whatever that means."

"Oh, come on, Igor, spit it out."

Still, Igor remained quiet as leaned over and knocked one of the few remaining billiard balls into a hole on the side of the table. "I would be interested in Anastasia if I thought the family would let me marry her," he said finally, naming the youngest of Alexei's four older sisters.

Konstantin's eyebrows furrowed as he contemplated his brother's answer. Behind him, Pilar smiled. "I like Anastasia," she said. "She's funny."

Igor nodded. "She's been the prankster in the family ever since we were children," he said. "It always worried Nicholas and Alexandra, because they never knew whether she would offend someone, but I always thought she was funny."

Konstantin nodded in agreement. "Alexandra was always stuffy," he said. "Anastasia was always a breath of fresh air."

Igor sighed. "I'm not sure they'd let me marry her, though," he said. "Alexandra is pretty set on international matches for all four girls. It looks like Marie might stay in Russia, and Alexandra isn't happy about it. She's thinking of trying to match Anastasia with a British prince."

"Maybe you should talk to Alyosha rather than to Alexandra," Konstantin suggested. "At least he'd take you seriously."

"Maybe," Igor said. He didn't sound convinced, but instead of saying anything further, he leaned over the billiard table and took one last shot. A second later, the eight-ball disappeared into the far corner of the table.

# A BROTHER'S PAIN

Konstantin looked down the formal dining table at his childhood palace of Pavlovsk and smiled. He and his brothers and sisters had all gathered for dinner, bringing their spouses but leaving their children in the care of their governesses. On one end, his sisters Vera and Tatiana chattered away. As he watched, his wife Pilar got up and joined them. Soon, she was laughing away with her sisters-in-law. *I'm happy Pilar fits in so well with the family*, Konstantin thought. *I've loved her for a long time.*

Next to Pilar, Konstantin's oldest brother, Ioann, and his youngest brother, George, discussed George's desire to visit America as he served in Russia's navy. Their brother Gavril interjected the occasional joke into the conversation.

*Only Igor is unengaged*, Konstantin thought as he watched his younger brother. Igor sat directly across from him, and was pushing food around his plate without really eating it. *He's not really listening to the conversation, either*, Konstantin thought. He picked up one of the only remaining items on his plate, a small tomato, and threw it at Igor.

Igor looked startled as the tomato hit him. "Yuck," he said when he realized what had happened. He picked the tomato up from where it had fallen on his lap and put it on his plate. "Why'd you do that?"

"To bring you back to the present," Konstantin said.

Igor shrugged and put down his fork and knife. "I'm really not hungry," he said.

Konstantin looked down the table and saw that everyone's plate was empty except Igor's. In a second, Gavril was eying Igor, and it was clear that he'd heard the conversation. "Igor, are you feeling alright?" Gavril asked. "I've never seen you eat so little."

"I'm fine," Igor said curtly.

Konstantin and Gavril glanced at each other. Then they looked back at Igor.

Once the dinner dishes had been cleared, the siblings adjourned to one of the drawing rooms. Igor went to one of the windows and stared out as his siblings settled into the comfortable chairs around the room. Konstantin lit a cigarette, and Ioann and Gavril followed suit. Konstantin allowed Igor one more minute by himself at the window before he stood up and went over to him.

Both brothers stood at the window for awhile, looking out at the familiar view outside the window. Then Konstantin glanced behind him and saw that Gavril and Ioann were watching him. The rest of their siblings and spouses were sitting around and talking.

"Igor," Konstantin finally said, dropping an arm around his brother's shoulders. "What's on your mind?"

"Who said I have anything on my mind?" Igor replied with a shrug.

"Oh, come on, Igor," Ioann said from behind them. He and Gavril stood and joined Konstantin and Igor at the window.

Konstantin dropped his arm to his side and watched as Igor's teeth clenched. To his shock, he saw tears forming in Igor's eyes. "What happened?" he asked.

"I've been spending too much time at the Winter Palace," Igor replied.

"How's that possible?" Gavril said. "You're Alyosha's ADC. You're *supposed* to be there."

Igor shrugged. "I was doing it partly because of Anastasia too," he said.

Konstantin was suddenly reminded of his conversation with Igor several months before. "Did you ever discuss your interest with Alyosha?" he asked.

"I didn't have to," Igor replied. His tears started to overflow. "Alexandra realized I was interested. She told me to meet with her yesterday, so of course I did."

"In her Mauve Buodoir?" Gavril asked, slightly sarcastically.

*He's never liked Alexandra, or her furnishings,* Konstantin thought. He looked back at Igor, who was nodding.

"I knew something was wrong, right away," Igor said. "If it were state business, she would have waited for Alyosha in his study." He sniffed and wiped his tears away with his hand.

"What did she say?" Konstantin asked. Pilar suddenly appeared at his side, and the rest of his siblings, realizing something was wrong, had gathered around and were listening to Igor's narration.

Igor shrugged, and his tears continued flowing. "She said I wasn't good enough for Anastasia, especially now that Alyosha has allowed Marie to remain in Russia to marry." Igor shook his head. "She said that if I'd been a Grand Duke, maybe she would have considered it, but even then, I'd probably lose out to a foreign prince, especially once that was in line for a throne."

"That's ridiculous," Ioann said. "We're the first generation that didn't get the Grand Ducal title."

"Screw her," Konstantin added. "You're more than worthy of Anastasia's hand in marriage."

Igor shook his head again, and his tears continued to flow down his face. "I've never been good enough," he said. "Alexandra made that clear. How could I ever have thought otherwise?"

Ioann put his arm around Igor's shoulders. "That's not true at all," he said.

Konstantin felt his insides twisting. *This is how I felt after I was denied Elizabeth's hand in marriage,* he thought. *Why does this keep happening to our family? Are we cursed?* He took a deep breath. "I agree with Ioann," he said. "You'd make a fine husband, and Anastasia is missing out."

"Did you speak with Anastasia herself at all about marrying her?" Tatiana asked.

Igor shook his head. "I always thought she was interested in me, but I never got to say anything to her directly."

"Would you consider talking to Alyosha about it?" George asked, pained by his older brother's tears. "He's more reasonable than his mother."

*I suggested Igor do that the last time we talked about Igor's interest in Anastasia,* Konstantin thought. *Maybe Igor could have avoided all of this by acting faster.*

But Igor shook his head again and sighed. "I probably should have done that to start with, before Alexandra had her say," Igor said. "I don't have a chance now."

Konstantin put his hand on Igor's shoulder. "I'm not sure I agree with that," he said. "But maybe it couldn't hurt to examine other marriage prospects as well."

Igor just shrugged.

*I hope he listens to that suggestion,* Konstantin thought. *It would really be a shame for him to spend his life as a bachelor.*

"I also think it's a good idea to think of other prospects, Igor," Gavril said.

Igor simply clenched his teeth again and stared out the window.

Ioann looked around the room at his crestfallen siblings. Then he looked back at Igor and took a deep breath. "I really don't want to send you home in this condition," he said. "Do you want to stay here for the night?"

Slowly, Igor nodded. "I think that's a good idea."

The next morning, Konstantin called Pavlovsk at an early hour, hoping to talk to Igor before he went to work at the Winter Palace. "How are you feeling?" he asked when Igor got on the phone.

"Better," Igor admitted. "But I'm sorry about last night. Everyone else was having such a good time, and I ruined it."

"That's not true," Konstantin said. "We all care about you. If you're having a problem, we want to know about it."

Still, when he hung up, Konstantin felt a certain amount of sadness. *I really want him to be happy,* he thought. *Maybe I should start looking into other princesses for him. I'd be happy to at least get him thinking about who's eligible. He really needs to make the choice on his own, though.*

Pilar appeared at the door of his study. "Did you speak to Igor?" she asked.

Konstantin nodded. "He's feeling better."

"I feel bad for him," Pilar said, coming into the room and sitting in a chair across from her husband. "I certainly know what it's like to feel as though you'll spend the rest of your life alone."

"As do I," Konstantin agreed. "It's not a feeling I'd wish on anybody else."

# STEADY DYNASTY

It was May 18, 1922. Konstantin took a deep breath as he stood in the Petrovsky Palace. His nerves were jangling so loudly he was sure they drowned out the cacophony of bells that were ringing across Moscow. Then he eyed Pilar, who was holding their younger son, two-month-old Boris.

"Relax, Kostya," Pilar said when she caught him eyeing her. "Everything will be fine."

Ioann, Elena and their children joined them. Ioann held his youngest child, Vyacheslav, who was just over a year old. Konstantin smiled as his little nephew. Then he looked down at his older son, the nearly three-year-old Sergei, who sat at his feet, playing with the laces on his boots. Vyacheslav looked at Sergei and squirmed in Ioann's arms. Ioann put him on the floor next to Sergei, and the two boys started playing together, grinning and babbling.

Konstantin almost felt himself relaxing as his mother and the rest of his siblings joined them. "Well, this is certainly incredible," he said. "I never thought Alyosha would live long enough to become tsar, but here were are in Moscow for his coronation."

"Oh ye of little faith," Igor said with a grin. "Alyosha's had his bumps and his bruises, but he's also been trying to take care of himself. He wants this coronation to happen quite badly."

Just then, a commotion outside announced the arrival of Alexei's procession from the train station. Konstantin and Ioann simultaneously scooped up Sergei and Vyacheslav and made a dash for the window. Outside, Konstantin could see the towering Grand Duke Nicholas Nikolaievich, well over two meters tall, dismounting from his horse. Behind him, Alexei's carriage was surrounded by the honor guard of an Uhlan regiment whose helmet plumes swayed in the wind.

Konstantin's heart beat faster as Nicholas went to open Alexei's carriage door. Next to him, Pilar was watching with interest. *This is her first coronation,* Konstantin thought. Outside, Alexei stepped from the carriage, grinning, and Konstantin felt his heart swell with pride. *Alyosha may just get through this event after all,* he thought.

Three days later, Konstantin's eyes were wide as he entered the Petrovsky Palace again. It was noon, and the bright sun poured down. Already, Konstantin could feel sweat beginning to form on his brow, *and the procession into Moscow proper hasn't even started yet.* He was glad for the cooler insides of the Palace, and was relieved to see that the extended imperial family was gathering, right on time. Konstantin joined Alexei's four sisters- Olga, Tatiana, Marie and Anastasia- and was glad to see them altogether again.

When Alexei appeared, however, Konstantin gasped in horror. He knew the young tsar had been following the church's custom of fasting for the last three days, but still he was unprepared for Alexei's pale countenance and drawn appearance. Large gray bags were under his eyes, and Konstantin had the urge to force Alexei to lie down and eat something.

"I hope he can do this," George said doubtfully from next to Konstantin. Konstantin shot his youngest brother a look of unease and nodded.

A few minutes before one, Alexei gathered the family's Grand Dukes and Princes together for one last conferring. When he was certain that everything was ready, the family got into place, and procession began. Long rows of Cossacks and Astrakhan Kubans rode out, heading for the Kremlin. They were followed by a multitude of horsemen, each dressed in competing colors. Then, a single cannon shot roared, and Konstantin knew that it was the signal that Alexei had appeared on the steps of the Petrovsky Palace. He craned to see his young cousin among the thousands of people that were there, but even from the vantage place of his tall horse, Konstantin could only see the top of Alexei's head.

A second cannon blast reverberated against the Palace walls, and Konstantin knew that Alexei was mounting the large white horse that had been brought to him. As he waited for the third cannon blast, which signaled that Alexei had ridden out through the gates of the Palace up ahead of him, Konstantin looked at his brothers and grinned. In unison, they grinned back. Then the cannon fired a third time, and Konstantin, Igor, Ioann, Gavril and George, surrounded by the rest of the family's Princes and Grand Dukes, rode through the gates behind their young tsar.

*This is great,* Konstantin thought, his face stretched from its smile. The cheers of the thousands of people around him overwhelmed him. Then the bells from Moscow's thousand churches all began to peal in unison, and Konstantin was sure he was about to go deaf. Next to him, his brothers all wore similar expressions of wonder and pride. Konstantin thought of Pilar, being driven in one of the carriages with the other women in the family. *I know she's enjoying this,* he thought. *We're going to be telling stories about this for the rest of our lives.*

"Whoa," Igor said suddenly.

Konstantin looked over at him and saw him staring upwards. He followed his brother's gaze and saw a flock of doves flying overhead. *A good omen,* Konstantin thought as the procession continued towards the Kremlin. *Maybe Alyosha will have a long reign after all.*

All along the route, Konstantin kept one eye on the horsemen in front of him, and one eye on the scenery around him. Every building had been decorated profusely, and banners of every color sang out happily. Banners and icons of Alexei were everywhere. The windows of most buildings were thrown open, and Konstantin could see people packed at each window, straining to get a glimpse of the procession. The sheer number of people around him was nearly overwhelming. *This ride wouldn't take long on a normal day,* he thought. *But this procession will easily take over two hours.*

When the procession finally reached the Kremlin, Konstantin was glad to see the red brick walls, glad to get inside to the coolness of the Uspensky Sobor. The service, once it started, also had a calming effect on Konstantin as he breathed in the smell of incense and breathed slowly in tune with the priests' familiar chanting. Still, he kept an eye on Alexei, tall and pale. *He still looks regal, despite it all,* Konstantin thought. When Alexei recited the Nicene Creed, Konstantin was impressed by how his strong voice filled the cathedral.

Then Alexei disappeared into the church's inner sanctum by himself for a few minutes, and Konstantin looked over at his family. Pilar was smiling, and Sergei was staring around in wonder. *Sergei has been so quiet that I forgot he was here,* Konstantin thought as he took his son from Pilar. Then he looked over at his siblings.

Vera looked back at him and grinned. "This is incredible," she whispered. Konstantin nodded in agreement.

When Alexei returned, the service continued until it was finished. When the service was over, Konstantin lined up behind his mother and siblings to greet and congratulate Alexei. He watched with amusement as Vsevolod, Ioann's oldest son, bowed and kissed Alexei's hand. "I'm so glad I've gotten to be your ADC all this time," Konstantin heard Igor say to Alexei.

*He means it, too,* Konstantin thought. Then he glanced behind him in time to see Princess Ileana of Romania standing on tiptoes trying to see around him and his brothers. "You'll need to grow a couple of meters before you can do that," he teased her. "My older brothers are some of the tallest princes in Alexei's kingdom."

"That's probably true," Ileana replied earnestly, and they both laughed.

When it came time for Konstantin to offer his congratulations to Alexei, he felt his words stick in his throat. "Congratulations, Alyosha," he managed to say. "I'm quite pleased to be here. Everything has been magnificent." *I wish I were better with words,* he thought. But Alexei smiled at him, and Konstantin could he was genuinely happy and relieved that so much of the coronation was now over.

"Yes, this whole service has been so moving," Ioann added.

"Ioann's had tears coming down his face the whole time," Konstantin joked. *I can't help but tease him,* he thought. *Anything religious moves him that way.*

But Alexei's grin remained unabated. "It is so good to have you all here," he said.

Later that night, Ioann, Igor, Gavril and George all came by Konstantin's apartments. *I'm glad we're all staying here,* he thought. *I definitely want to go out and see the entertainments that Alyosha scheduled for the city.* As he looked at Pilar, though, he could see her starting to yawn. "Why don't you go to sleep, honey?" he asked. "Sergei and Boris are already asleep, and I think they'll stay that way for awhile."

Ioann nodded at his sister-in-law. "Elena decided to turn in too, and my kids are all asleep."

"I'm surprised," Gavril said. "Didn't Vsevolod want to go out?"

"He's coming to the opera with us tomorrow," Ioann replied. "Besides, now that the actual coronation service is over, we'll be spending tomorrow and the next day enjoying all of the festivities."

Pilar looked at Konstantin and nodded as she suppressed another yawn. "I'm not going to make it through any of the festivities tonight," she said. "But I think you should go out with your brothers."

"Are you sure you'll be alright?" Konstantin asked.

Pilar nodded. "And Elena is right downstairs if I need anything."

"Alright," Konstantin said as he grabbed his jacket. Then he looked at his brothers. "Let's go."

That night, long after the ballet they had attended was over and they had eaten supper, the five brothers walked through the streets of Moscow, enjoying the revelry of the citizens around them. Konstantin drew a flask of vodka from his coat, and was pleased that it contained the Imperial coat of arms. Next to him, Igor was pulling a similar flask from his own jacket. He grinned at Konstantin, and the two brothers clinked their flasks together in a toast. Ioann, Gavril and George looked over at them and smiled too.

All at once, a loud bang shook the air. Konstantin jumped. Then he remembered to look upwards, and saw fireworks exploding across the sky in all colors. "Wow!" he gasped. His neck craned forward to see each band of fireworks as the red, orange and yellow flames careened across the sky.

"That is awesome," Igor said matter-of-factly.

"I heard Alyosha was planning multiple sets of fireworks," George said. "I'll bet we missed a bunch of them while we were in the ballet."

"If I'd known that, I might have stayed outside," Konstantin joked.

"Well, we're seeing them now," Gavril said as his head remained turned upward.

Loud cheers followed each round of fireworks, and Konstantin could not keep the smile from his face. *I'm in*

*Moscow for the crowning of the Tsar,* he thought. *What a time to be Russian.*

# HIDDEN OPPORTUNITIES

Only a few weeks after Alexei's coronation, word went around that a British delegation, headed by King George himself, would be visiting St. Petersburg the following week. "Alyosha said he's trying to get the British to invest in our economy and infrastructure," Prince Igor Konstantinovich said to his brother Konstantin as they arrived at the Mariinsky Theater in St. Petersburg.

"I think that's wise," Konstantin replied. He exited their carriage and gave his hand to his wife Pilar, feeling the confines of his starched military uniform as he did so. "It's no secret that our railroads and supply lines were a mess during the Great War, and that it hindered our ability to fight."

Igor nodded as he exited the carriage and closed the door behind him. "Alyosha is looking for long-term investment."

Konstantin, Pilar and Igor turned to go inside the theater. Behind them, the carriage rode off down the street, and its wheels joined the cacophony of the horses' hooves on the cobblestones. The brothers' military decorations sparkled in the light of the gas lamps in front of the theater as they walked up the steps to the entrance, and Pilar's diamond necklace did the same.

"I think Alyosha is pretty wise in that regard, despite how young he is," Konstantin said as they reached the entrance to the theater.

All around them, young officers snapped into salutes, and civilians bowed and curtseyed. Konstantin, Pilar and Igor responded in kind as they made their way to the family's box to watch the ballet.

Igor nodded at his brother as they reached their box. "I was really scared for Alyosha, taking the throne at 16," he said.

"So was I," Konstantin admitted. "Even at his coronation, I thought he looked really young."

"He's still only eighteen," Igor replied.

"I thought he looked regal at the coronation anyway," Pilar said. "I was impressed by how he carried himself."

Inside the family's box, Konstantin and Igor's oldest brother, Ioann, was already there with his wife Elena and their oldest son, eight-year-old Vsevolod. Vsevolod grinned when he saw his uncles and aunt. "Mama and Papa let me come to the ballet tonight," he said. "It's my first time." He rubbed his hands together with delight.

Konstantin grinned at his nephew. Vsevolod was wearing a child's version of a Russian army uniform, and he had obviously tried to look older by having his hair slicked back. *He's so cute,* Konstantin thought. "Ioann said you've been looking forward to this for weeks," he said.

Vsevolod nodded as Konstantin and Pilar took their seats. His grin remained unabated. Then he went over to where Igor was sitting. Pilar shot Konstantin an amused look. "He's so cute," she said.

Konstantin laughed and nodded. *She can definitely read my mind,* he thought.

"Uncle Igor, all Mama and Papa have been talking about is the British delegation that's coming next week," Vsevolod said. "Can we talk about something else?"

"Kostya and I were just discussing the British delegation as well," Igor replied. "I think we're as boring as your parents."

Vsevolod made a face at him before picking up a program and sitting down to read it.

Ioann sent his son an amused glance as he sat down between Konstantin and Igor. "I suspect the British have more in mind that just state business," he said.

*Maybe Ioann can read my mind too*, Konstantin thought as he glanced at Igor. *I've been certain that George is going to talk to Alyosha about a marriage between Anastasia and one of his sons ever since the British announced they were coming. I hope this visit doesn't upset Igor too much.*

Two seats away, Igor was sighing. "Alexandra has wanted a British match for Anastasia since we were kids," he said. "Even Anastasia is aware of it, and doesn't seem to be opposed."

"Well, then perhaps it's something you need to come to terms with," Ioann said.

*I agree, even if I may not have said it so harshly*, Konstantin thought.

Igor just shrugged. "What?" he said a minute later, when he found his brothers and sisters-in-law staring at him. "What were you expecting me to say? It's not like I have any other prospects."

"Maybe Anastasia's wedding will change that," Konstantin said. "I'm sure that royal families from all across Europe will be there."

"We'll see," Igor replied. "We don't even know that there will be a wedding."

At that moment, the lights in the theater dimmed, and the music began. Konstantin faced forward. *Igor can't go on being so grumpy about this*, he thought, even as he remembered his brother's tears at Alexandra's rejection. Then Konstantin shook his head at himself as ballerinas poured onto the stage in front of him. *It took you nine years to marry Pilar after you were rejected by Elizabeth*, he thought. *Try to have more sympathy for Igor.*

He swallowed. *It won't take Igor that long to find someone else. I'll make sure of that.*

Ten days later, Konstantin got the news he'd been expecting: Prince Henry of England had proposed to Anastasia, and she had accepted. That night, Konstantin and Pilar made sure to visit Igor at his mansion on the Nevsky Prospect. To Konstantin's surprise, they found Ioann and Gavril already there. Konstantin was less surprised to find Igor sitting in one of his favorite armchairs, tears rolling down his face.

"What would you know about it?" Igor was saying to Gavril as Konstantin and Pilar entered the room. "You're already married to Nina, and you didn't even get the Tsar's permission to do it."

*Actually, I haven't seen Nina for awhile,* Konstantin thought. *I've been wondering what's been going on.*

"No, as a matter of fact, we've been separated for awhile," Gavril said. "I filed for divorce months ago, and it's nearly final."

"What?" Konstantin, Igor and Ioann all said at the same time. "Why?"

*What's going on with our family?* Konstantin wondered. *Why is it that half of us can't settle down with eligible brides?*

Gavril shrugged, and pain seemed to emanate from him too. "I wanted children, and it wasn't happening. Besides, she wanted to continue her dancing career, and children would have prevented that." He stopped speaking and clenched his teeth for a second. "I hope that marriage hasn't done away with my chances with a princess of our station."

"You should have thought of that before you married her," Igor said, slapping his hands down on his chair's armrests and standing up. He shook his head. "How about I skip Anastasia's wedding altogether? Nobody will know the difference. Alexandra might even be happy about it."

Konstantin shook his head, and was glad to see Ioann, Gavril and Pilar doing the same. "Skipping the wedding would be an insult to the whole family, not just Alexandra," Konstantin said. "And besides, you shouldn't let Alexandra get under your skin anymore."

"How am I supposed to do that, Kostya?" Igor demanded. "I work for Alyosha, and she's his mother."

"She's been taking less of an active role in society than Dowager Empresses usually do," Ioann counseled. "Let's just see what happens."

"Promise me you'll go to the wedding?" Konstantin said. "I really don't think you should skip it."

"Fine," Igor said curtly.

Despite Igor's unhappiness, Konstantin thought the matter was resolved- until the night before the family was supposed to travel to England. Konstantin and Pilar joined Konstantin's siblings at Pavlovsk, and they all planned on departing from there early the next morning. Long after the sun dipped below the horizon, however, Igor still hadn't returned from the Winter Palace.

"I'm concerned about him," Konstantin admitted to his wife and siblings. "I know Mama thinks he's just working late-" Konstantin glanced into the next room to make sure his mother wasn't listening- "but I'm afraid there's something more going on."

"Do you think he'd really skip out on the wedding, though?" George asked. "It's not like him."

"You didn't hear the conversation we had when the engagement was announced," Gavril said. "He was thinking of skipping it even then." He shook his head. "I don't like this at all." There was a minute of silence as everyone looked at each other. Then Gavril picked up the phone on the table next to him and dialed the Winter Palace. "Hello, Alyosha," he said when Alexei picked up the phone. "It's Gavril. We've been expecting Igor back here for some time now."

"I sent him home awhile ago," Alexei replied, and Konstantin could hear his voice coming through the receiver. "Are you sure he isn't back at Pavlovsk?"

"I'm sure," Gavril replied, frowning.

*Where in hell could Igor be?* Konstantin wondered. *I don't like this at all.*

"Please send him home if you find him," Gavril said into the phone. "We're all supposed to leave for England together in the morning." He hung up the phone and looked at his siblings. "Alyosha's going to look for him at the Winter Palace."

There was a silence as everyone in the room stood there, looking at each other. After a minute, Konstantin went to the window, wondering if he would be able to see a carriage finally bringing his brother home. He stood there for nearly an hour, his teeth clenched. *Is it possible he wasn't at the Winter Palace?* Konstantin wondered. *Where else could he be? We told him to come here when he was done with work, not to go back to his own home.*

Then the sound of a carriage clattered outside the palace, and Konstantin jumped. He looked outside, and through the window of the carriage, he could see Igor sitting inside. *Finally,* Konstantin thought as he went outside to greet his brother. As he walked, he saw the Romanov family's imperial crest on the side of the carriage. *Alyosha must have sent Igor here in one of his own carriages,* he realized, and the thought was reinforced when he recognized the driver as one who was attached to the Winter Palace.

The driver stifled a yawn as Igor threw the carriage door open and unfolded his body onto the street. He didn't even close the door behind him as he rushed into the palace. He didn't look at Konstantin either. "Igor, wait," Konstantin said, but his brother gave no indication that he'd heard him. In a minute, he had disappeared into Pavlovsk.

Konstantin, looking through one of the front windows of the palace, could see Gavril, Ioann and George greeting Igor. Gavril in particular was holding out a hand towards Igor's chest to prevent his younger brother's flight further inside. Konstantin looked back at the carriage that Igor had just exited. "Sorry," he said to the driver as he closed the carriage door.

The driver's exhausted expression didn't change, and Konstantin couldn't fault him.

*It is after midnight,* Konstantin thought. He dug into his pockets and pulled out several rubles, which he handed to the driver.

"Thanks," the driver responded, and soon the carriage was clattering back towards downtown St. Petersburg.

Konstantin went back inside Pavlovsk to find that Igor had already gone upstairs to the apartments that he shared with George. George had followed him, and Gavril and Ioann had let them go. Their mother, Elizaveta, and their sisters Tatiana and Vera had joined them in the drawing room, tears filling their eyes.


The next morning, as the family left for England, Konstantin's mind was already working. In London, the wedding ceremony was held in Westminster Abbey, and Konstantin was impressed by how beautiful both the setting and the ceremony were. As Anastasia and Henry recited their vows, Konstantin looked over at Igor. His eyes were dry, and he was paying attention to the ceremony. *Good for him,* Konstantin thought. *He's pulled himself together a little bit, at least. I was worried that he wouldn't even be able to do that much.*

When the ceremony was over, the guests were taken to Buckingham Palace for the reception in horse-drawn carriages. All along the route, British citizens lined the route and cheered. Konstantin, riding in a carriage with Pilar, George and Vera, smiled at the noise. When their carriage arrived at the palace, the four of them went inside, and Vera, seeing Anastasia's three sisters nearby, scampered over to join them.

Konstantin used his sister's departure as an opportunity to sneak over to the large hall where the reception would be held. Pilar and George followed him, and George eyed his older brother. "You're planning something, aren't you?" he said. "I know that look."

A secretive smile came over Konstantin's features as he snuck a glance into the large hall through a door that was swinging shut after an exiting servant. The swift scan confirmed that the room was empty, and Konstantin took the opportunity to dash inside. In a second, Pilar and George were following him. Pilar was grinning, but George looked worried. "What are you doing?" George hissed. "We're not supposed to be in here yet."

"Sssshhhh!" Konstantin hissed back as he scanned the huge list of where the guests were sitting. Despite the thousands of guests that were attending, Konstantin soon found his name. *Igor, Gavril, Pilar and I are all at the same table,* he thought. *Who are the other four people sitting with us?* He saw the names of an Italian princess and a French princess. *Okay, that's fine,* he thought, *but there's no way I'm sitting with those two old British counts.* He pulled a pen from his pocket and started changing the table numbers next to the counts' names.

"Kostya, stop it!" George said.

"Sshhh," Pilar said. She looked over her husband's shoulder at the changes he was making. When he was finished, they both dashed to Table Numbers 11 and 12, and exchanged the small nametags from those tables onto Table 5, where they would be sitting. When they were finished, the two old counts had been moved to Tables 11 and 12, and Princess Sophie of Hohenberg and Lady Maud Louisa Emma, daughter of the Duke of Devonshire, were seated at Table 5.

George waved at Konstantin and Pilar to hurry as they rushed back to the door. They ducked back into the hallway outside the reception room and found their mother standing with their sisters. Elizaveta Mavrikievna eyed them. "What were you doing in there?" she asked.

"Just trying to figure out where we'll be sitting," Konstantin said.

Elizaveta shook her head at him. "You shouldn't have been in there," she said. "You have to wait until the bride and groom lead their guests in."

"Sorry, Mama," Konstantin replied. As soon as his mother turned away, Konstantin and Pilar exchanged a look and struggled to contain their laughter.

When the reception started, Konstantin and Pilar hung back a bit to allow Igor and Gavril to get seated among the princesses at their table. When they finally approached the table, Igor was seated in between Sophie and Maud. Gavril sat in between Maud and Princess Lucia Maria Raniera of Bourbon-Two Sicilies. Princess Anne of Orleans was the table's last occupant. For a moment, everyone just looked at each other. Then Pilar broke the silence by introducing herself.

"So you're Anastasia's cousins," Maud said when Konstantin, Gavril and Igor had introduced themselves. The three brothers nodded. "We've been wondering what she's like since her engagement to Henry was announced."

"She's funny," Igor said.

Konstantin nodded, glad that Igor seemed to be coming out of his shell, if only a little. Nearly an hour into the reception, Igor was laughing and joking around with both Maud and Sophie, and Konstantin felt justified in having changed their seats. Then he looked up to see Alexei, who had been making his rounds greeting people and was now approaching his table. Upon seeing Alexei, Maud, Sophie, Anne and Lucia fell into an uncomfortable silence.

*He is the Russian Tsar*, Konstantin thought. *It's no wonder they're intimidated by him, but they really shouldn't be. He's young, and he's good with people.* "Alyosha, did you meet any of these ladies at your coronation?" Konstantin broke the silence by asking.

Alexei frowned as he thought about it. "I may have met Pilar before that," he said. "Maybe at your wedding, Kostya?"

Konstantin shook his head at his cousin. "And here I was, expecting a serious answer," he said.

Alexei's face lit up with the grin that Konstantin knew so well. Then Anastasia appeared next to her brother. Alexei draped his arm around his sister and continued smiling.

Anastasia looked around at the table in front of her, and Konstantin could see a slight frown on her face as she realized that the seating was slightly different than she remembered. But she didn't say anything, and the frown disappeared into a smile as she and Alexei began cracking jokes. Konstantin watched Igor and Gavril laugh in response, saw Sophie and Maud join their laughter.

Soon, Konstantin felt a smile growing on his face too.

# SETTLING DOWN

Shortly after Christmas, 1922, Konstantin and Pilar visited Gavril at the Marble Palace and found him packing his trunks. "Going somewhere?" Konstantin asked, bewildered. *I didn't know Gavril was planning on traveling.*

Gavril nodded. "I'm going back to London," he said. "Alyosha has been discussing military matters with King George, especially military education, and I'm happy to add my expertise."

Konstantin nodded. "You'll be of great use," he said.

"I like London," Pilar added. "I might have gone with you if I'd had more advance notice of your trip."

Gavril smiled. "I like London too," he said. "But I'll only be there a week. I won't even be gone long enough for you to miss me."

"That's certainly true," Konstantin replied with a grin. Gavril gave him a punch in the arm, and they both laughed.

More than a week later, on New Year's Eve, Konstantin, Pilar, Sergei and Boris headed for the Winter Palace to spend the holiday with Alexei. "It must be pretty quiet in the Palace now that Marie and Anastasia are married and living somewhere else, and Alexandra has retired to a convent," Pilar said.

Konstantin nodded. "I think it's great that Alexei is trying to connect with the extended family, though," he said. "Nicholas and Alexandra were always so focused on their children."

When they arrived at the Winter Palace, Alexei, Igor and Gavril were exiting Alexei's study and heading for the Palace's church. It was only then that Konstantin remembered that Gavril had had an audience with Alexei about his trip to London.

"Congratulations," Alexei was saying to Gavril as Konstantin and Pilar got within earshot. "I'm glad it worked out."

"What happened?" Konstantin asked.

"Maud and I have been corresponding since we met at Anastasia's wedding," Gavril replied. "I asked her to marry me while I was in London."

"And she accepted, obviously," Alexei said.

"We're thinking of having the wedding in June," Gavril added.

Konstantin eyed his older brother as they all headed to the church. "You certainly play a close hand," he said.

Gavril looked back at him, his eyebrows coming together in a frown. "What do you mean?"

"I didn't even know you were writing to Maud," he said. "And when we discussed your trip to London, you didn't say anything about proposing to her."

Gavril shrugged. "I had Alyosha's permission, and Mama's."

"Mama kept it quiet too, then. I didn't hear anything about it from her."

"I asked her to keep it quiet."

"Playing your cards close."

"Please don't be angry with me, Kostya," Gavril begged. "I just wasn't sure it would work out, so I didn't want everyone to know it was happening."

"I'm not *angry*, Gavrilushka," Konstantin replied, hearing the sound of their boots striking the palace's parquet floor as they walked towards the church. "Just miffed. This is an important step. I would have liked to have heard about it."

When they got to the church, Alexei made a beeline for the iconostasis and knelt. Gavril followed him. Konstantin and Pilar hung back, remaining at the back of the church.

Igor joined them. "I had no idea he was going to propose to Maud either," he said. "He must have waited to ask Alyosha's permission for when I wasn't in the room."

Konstantin nodded. "He was definitely secretive about it."

Igor shook his head. "I don't plan on acting the same way."

Both Konstantin and Pilar eyed Igor. "Are you thinking of Sophie?" Konstantin asked. Igor nodded. "See, at least I knew you were writing to her."

Igor nodded again. "I don't plan on going alone either when I go to propose to her," he said.

At that moment, the rest of their family began coming into the church- first Ioann and Elena and their children, then Elizaveta Mavrikievna with George and Vera. Tatiana and her children were close behind them.

Konstantin looked back at Igor. "Find me when the service is over, and we can talk about it some more."

After the service, and the huge dinner banquet, the family bundled up and went out on to the roof of the Winter Palace to watch the fireworks that were being set off all across the city. Konstantin made sure to join Igor at the side of the roof, and together they looked out over the Neva River. Konstantin felt the bitter air dig into his skin as he stared at ice on the Neva, which reflected the lamps along it.

"So you're thinking of going to Vienna?" Konstantin asked, picking up on their earlier conversation as Pilar and Tatiana joined them.

Igor nodded. "Sophie certainly seems amenable to a proposal. Even at Anastasia's wedding, she said that she'd been engaged to some German count, but that he'd broken it off."

"I remember that," Konstantin said. *Guess there's a lot of that going around.*

Igor shrugged. "At least it gives me an opportunity that I wouldn't have had otherwise."

Overhead, the fireworks suddenly started, and Konstantin ducked involuntarily at the sound. Igor did too. Glancing behind him, Konstantin could see that Ioann and Gavril were also bracing themselves against the assault of sound, light and color. Behind them, Konstantin could see Sergei standing with Ioann and Tatiana's kids, staring at the sky in wonder. He smiled.

Then Alexei appeared in Konstantin's line of sight, holding a bottle of vodka and a number of glasses. Still smiling, Konstantin took one from him, and Alexei made his rounds until all the adults held shots of vodka. "Cheers," Alexei said as he raised his glass.

"Cheers," Konstantin replied, and heard his brothers and sisters join the refrain.

Sergei, seeing his parents drinking something, came over to investigate. "What is that, Papa?" he asked, pointing a little finger at Konstantin's empty glass.

Pilar laughed. "This is for the adults only," she said.

"Aww, Mama," Sergei replied. He looked at Konstantin pleadingly, hoping for a different answer.

But Konstantin shook his head. "Sorry, Sergei," he said. He watched, trying to control his laughter, as his son's mouth turned downward as he went to rejoin his cousins. Konstantin went back to where Igor was standing, looking out over the Neva, and was happy to see that his brother was smiling. Konstantin allowed a minute of silence before saying, "I'd go with you to Vienna if you want."

Igor looked over at him and nodded. "I'd like that."

"I'd go too," Tatiana said, and Konstantin was surprised by the offer.

"What about your kids?" Igor asked.

"I'm sure Mama would be willing to have them stay with her at Pavlovsk for a few days," Tatiana replied. "They're not babies anymore."

"Alright," Igor said. "I've already written to Sophie about going, and she said she's happy to have me. I might go as early as the week after next."

Konstantin and Tatiana nodded. "That's fine," Konstantin said. "I assume she's still staying at Artstetten Castle?"

Igor nodded at the mention of the castle of Prince Jaroslav von Thun und Hohenstein, who had cared for Sophie and her brothers since their parents' death. "I'm looking forward to it already," he said.

Two weeks later, Konstantin, Igor and Tatiana were on the train to Vienna. As the train steamed into the station, Konstantin put an arm around his brother. "Are you ready for this?" he asked.

Igor nodded. "I think it's the right choice."

"I think so too," Konstantin replied.

The next day, the trio went to Artstetten Castle, where they had lunch with Sophie, Jaroslav, and Sophie's two brothers, Maximilian and Ernst. After lunch, Konstantin, Tatiana, Jaroslav, Maximilian and Ernst took tea in one of the sitting rooms as Igor and Sophie walked down one of the paths that ran behind the castle. Many of the walking paths had been cleared of the snow, and Konstantin found himself wondering what the castle looked like in the summer and fall.

"We usually only use this place as a summer castle," Maximilian said to Konstantin and Tatiana as Jaroslav stood at the window, watching Igor and Sophie disappear down the path.

"But Sophie wanted to be here for this- she really likes it here," Ernst added. "She'd stay here all year round if we'd let her."

"It is beautiful here in the autumn, when the leaves change color," Maximilian said.

The conversation continued, but Konstantin found himself thinking of Igor. *I hope he uses this time alone with Sophie wisely,* he thought. *He shouldn't hesitate.*

It was more than an hour later before Igor and Sophie returned. Konstantin eyed Igor as he helped Sophie out of her coat and boots, trying to spot any clues from his brother's facial expressions and demeanor. *Come on Igor, spit it out,* he thought.

"So?" Jaroslav asked as Igor removed his own coat, and Konstantin had to suppress a smile at his impatience.

"Yes," Igor said, and now Konstantin could not suppress a smile at Igor's normally reserved self coming to the forefront.

Tatiana laughed at her brother. "How about a complete sentence, Igor?" she asked.

"Yes, I asked Sophie to marry me, and yes, she said yes," Igor said.

Konstantin started laughing too, certain that Igor would have thrown some object at Tatiana if there hadn't been other people in the room. "Congratulations," he said, standing up and embracing Igor. "I'm very happy for you."

Jaroslav smiled also as he embraced Sophie. Her brothers followed suit. "I'm happy too," Jaroslav said. "This has been a long time in the making."

*It hasn't been that long,* Konstantin thought. *They just met at Anastasia's wedding a few months ago. Pilar and I met eight years before we married. That's a long time.*

"When are you thinking of having the wedding?" Tatiana asked.

"We were discussing that," Igor said. "Gavril said he and Maud were shooting for June. I don't want to steal their thunder, but I'd hate to have to wait even longer than that."

Jaroslav nodded as he thought. "I think we could prepare something by April," he suggested.

Igor and Sophie looked at each other. "That would work for us," Igor said.

Konstantin grinned, and was relieved to see that not only did Igor smile back, but that his smile was reflected in the glow in his eyes. "We have to tell the rest of the family," Konstantin said. "They're all waiting to hear."

# A PROMISE MADE GOOD

Konstantin groaned silently as he held a golden nuptial crown over his brother Igor's head. Even with their brother George holding the other side of the crown, Konstantin still felt the weight of it. He looked over to where his last two brothers, Ioann and Gavril, held the other crown over the head of Igor's bride, Princess Sophie of Hohenberg. *They don't seem to be bothered by how heavy this thing is,* he thought.

The sweet smell of the incense hit Konstantin's nose mere seconds after the priests lit it. Then the smoke filled his throat, and Konstantin had to struggle to keep from coughing. *Dammit,* he thought. *Here I am, trying not to attract attention to myself, and yet I'm about to have a coughing fit that would interrupt the entire ceremony.*

Konstantin inhaled deeply, willing the incense to dislodge from his throat in the quietest way possible. When he was sure he could breathe smoothly again, he focused on the liturgy that the priests were chanting. It went on forever, and soon Konstantin was struggling to stay awake. It was only with a conscious effort that he managed to remain standing upright, holding the nuptial crown that was now thoroughly digging into his hands.

*God, I barely remember this stuff from my own wedding ceremony,* Konstantin thought. *I guess I was too focused on Pilar, and the fact that my wedding was finally happening. I wouldn't be surprised if Igor feels the same way later.*

When the ceremony was over, Konstantin was only too happy to head into the reception. More than two hours later, after he had danced as much as his feet would allow, he collapsed into a chair at a table with Pilar, Gavril, Maud, Ioann and Elena. Igor and Sophie continued dancing.

Pilar smiled at Konstantin as she held their younger son, Boris, on her lap. "Igor's finally happy," she said.

"Finally," Konstantin agreed.

Then, Alexei, smiling, joined their table. He nodded at Igor and Sophie, who were still dancing. "It's about time," he said, and Konstantin couldn't help but agree.

"So, what about you, Alyosha?" Ioann asked.

"What *about* me?" Alexei asked, looking over at him.

"Well, Igor's wedding is today, Gavril's wedding is in two months. Are you going to be next after that?"

Ioann sounded like he was slightly joking, but Konstantin thought the question was mostly serious. *Alyosha's only nineteen, but his hemophilia does make an early wedding even more necessary than a tsar's usually is.*

"I don't know yet," Alexei admitted. "Most of the eligible princesses are even younger than I am. It seems unfair to ask them to commit to such a thing at such a young age."

"Who are you thinking of?" Ioann pressed.

"Most of the eligible princesses," Alexei replied with a smile.

*Ioann's not going to get very far with this line of questioning,* Konstantin thought. *Alyosha is as good as playing his cards close as Gavril was when he was getting ready to propose to Maud.*

Then Alexei nodded towards Igor and Sophie. "Look," he said, directing the comment mostly at Konstantin and Pilar. "Sergei is joining the dancing."

Konstantin and Pilar looked over at their older son, who had just stepped out onto the dance floor and was trying to replicate Igor and Sophie's dance moves. After a minute, Sergei realized that he was failing miserably, and he looked quite unhappy.

Without hesitating, Konstantin burst into laughter, and Pilar joined him. The rest of the table followed suit. Soon, Konstantin was laughing so hard he felt his stomach muscles cramping, and was worried that the cramps would send his upper body forward and his face into his soup. He struggled to take a breath.

In front of him, Konstantin saw Igor struggling to contain a smile at his small nephew, but soon he too was unable to control his laughter. "Come here," Igor said to Sergei, breaking away from Sophie for a minute. Sophie was smiling too, and soon, all three of them were dancing in a circle.

# EXPANDED HORIZONS

Konstantin stood at the naval yard of Kronstadt, watching the hustle and bustle of sailors all around him. His wife and siblings all surrounded him, but still Konstantin felt out of sorts. He eyed his younger brother George, handsome and decked out in his naval uniform.

George grinned back at him. "Still not comfortable among all these sailors, Kostya?" he asked.

"I don't think any of us are," Ioann said. "You're the first of us to go into the Navy, Georgy."

"We Konstantinovichi brothers are definitely soldiers," Igor agreed. "You're making your own way here, George."

"All the way to America," Konstantin said. "It does seem very far away, I'll give you that."

"Alexei specifically wanted me to go on this trip when I started my service in the Navy," George said. "He was impressed by the American delegation at his coronation. He wanted to reciprocate in some fashion, and it's been almost a year since the coronation."

"Then he should have gone to America himself," Konstantin joked. *This is a long trip, and George will be going far away,* he thought. *He'll be traveling for over a month. It makes me nervous.*

"Alyosha is planning a trip there already," Igor said seriously.

Konstantin nodded. *Igor's been in on all of Alyosha's planning since he became his Aide-de-Camp,* he thought. *It's been good for both of them, and I am certainly glad to have someone that I trust watching out for Alyosha.*

Vera looked over at George. "Try not to stay away too long," she said. "The palace is going to be quiet without you."

George put his arm around Vera's shoulder as Kronstadt's whistle blew. "I'll miss you, too," he told his only younger sibling. "But maybe you'll make some new friends while I'm gone. That'll be easier when you're not in the shadow of someone of my caliber."

"Shut up," Vera said, pushing George away as everyone laughed.

But the whistle was the signal for the sailors to start boarding their ships, so George hugged his mother and all of his siblings. "Come home safely," Konstantin exhorted him.

"Relax, Kostya, we're not even going off to fight," George said. "This is more of a diplomatic, show-our-faces type of mission."

*He can only say that confidently because he was too young to fight in the Great War,* Konstantin thought. "Nevertheless," he said as George finished hugging the rest of the family goodbye. "I want you have a good time, but I want you back here in one piece."

"I will," George said seriously. Then he fell into line with his regiment, and soon Konstantin was watching him board the huge flagship that would take him to the United States.

Konstantin took Pilar's hand as he and the rest of his family watched the ships steam out of the harbor. When the ships were out of sight, the family turned to go back to their waiting motor cars. "I think this will be a good trip for George," Igor said as he and Sophie climbed into the same car as Konstantin and Pilar. "Even if it will be his first time away from home."

"I hope so," Konstantin said. "I hope so."

A month later, Konstantin was eager to see George after his return to Russia, but he had to wait until after George's regiment had met with Alexei. Konstantin shook his head in mock frustration when he heard that. "As if the tsar were more important than his brother," he said to Pilar.

"That's what happens when you're only a paltry prince," Pilar teased in reply.

Konstantin looked at her, and they both burst out laughing.

George's regiment went straight to Kronstadt after its audience with Alexei, so Konstantin and Pilar went there to find him. George met them for lunch at the officer's club on the base and then showed them his quarters. Konstantin smiled at the pile of souvenirs that George had acquired during his trip- small American flags, shot glasses, cigarette cases…

"What is this?" Konstantin asked, picking up a small purple envelope. The scent of lavender reached his nose, and a small, round object fell out of the envelope into his hand.

"Nothing," George said, quickly reaching out to grab both the envelope and the object that had been inside it.

Just as quickly, Konstantin hid them behind his back. He hadn't missed the shade of pink that George's face had turned- in fact, he thought it complemented the purple envelope quite nicely. Konstantin brought the small object around to his face to see what it was, and could see a portrait of a pretty young woman. "Aahhh, I see now," he said, a smile alighting on his features.

"Stop it!" George hissed, glancing around and hoping that no one from his regiment was around.

Pilar looked over Konstantin's shoulder to see the portrait, and she smiled too. "She's pretty," she said.

"Who is she?" Konstantin asked.

George's face went from pink to red. "I met her while I was in America."

"I might have surmised that on my own," Konstantin said, suppressing the desire to throw the portrait at his brother. "Does she have a name?"

"Grace Astor."

"Is she related to the Astor family of London?"

George nodded. "They're cousins."

"Maybe one of her British cousins would be a better match for you," Konstantin advised as he placed the envelope and portrait back with George's other souvenirs. "At least the Brits have titles and it would be considered an equal marriage."

George shrugged at that. "Even the American Astors have both money and a long lineage. Besides, I'm so far down in the succession that I can't imagine it would matter much."

"How old is Grace?" Pilar asked.

"Nineteen. She just finished her first year at Bryn Mawr College."

"That's almost British sounding," Konstantin said.

"It's a Welsh name, but the school is outside of Philadelphia," George replied.

"Why did she go there?" Konstantin asked, teasing slightly but also wanting to figure out just how much his brother had learned about this woman.

"Because it's a better school than Vassar and the other schools to which she was admitted," George said.

At that moment, other sailors from George's regiment entered the barracks. They snapped into a salute when they saw George and Konstantin. The two brothers saluted back, and then simultaneously moved towards the door of the barracks so that they could continue their conversation privately. Pilar followed, smiling at the sailors as they left.

"But she was interested enough in you to give you her portrait, and you were interested enough back to transport it all the way to Russia without losing it," Konstantin pressed his brother once they were outside the barracks.

"Even so, I think it would only be fair to let her finish her education," George said. "We'll see if we're still interested once she graduates. She's got another three years, and we're very far apart now."

Konstantin nodded. "I think that's a wise attitude," he said. "But I still think you should continue writing to her, nonetheless."

"Oh, I will," George said, a smile lighting up his face.

Konstantin smiled back. "Good," he said. "Maybe it will all work out in the end."

# MENDING FENCES

Konstantin looked up from the letter he was writing to see his brother Igor dashing into his study, waving a piece of paper and grinning. "Did you get one of these?" Igor asked, still grinning and speaking a bit too loudly.

Igor was still waving the paper around, so Konstantin had to discern its contents from its fancy writing, the color of its ink, and by the Romanov imperial double-headed eagle emblazoned on it. "If that's Alyosha's engagement announcement, then yes, I got one," Konstantin said with a smile, amused at his brother's excitement. "Did you tell Alyosha that you're this happy for him?"

"Oh come on, Kostya, of course I did," Igor said, swinging his arm until it connected with Konstantin's shoulder. "The wedding of a tsar!" he continued. "This is big news!"

"I know," Konstantin said, still smiling. "Even if Alyosha and Ileana are both a bit young."

"Yes, they are," Igor said, his smile disappearing slightly. "Alyosha said himself that he would have waited longer to marry, except for his hemophilia. Not even his doctors can tell him how long he'll live."

Konstantin sighed in frustration as he laid his pen on his desk. "I was afraid that was the case. He's only twenty, and Ileana is only sixteen. Marriage is a lot to ask of both of them."

Six months later, on the eve of the big wedding, Ileana made her grand entrance into St. Petersburg, and although Konstantin was part of the procession that led her carriage from the train station back to the Winter Palace, he wanted to make sure he had the chance to congratulate her in private before all the hoopla of the wedding. To do that, he kept an eye on the official list of people who were coming with their congratulations. One night, when nothing was on Ileana's schedule, he went to the Winter Palace unannounced and was led to her rooms by a servant who knew him, and whom Konstantin knew would keep quiet about the visit.

Once he was outside Ileana's door, Konstantin took a deep breath and stood up straight. He was about to knock when he heard Ileana talking to someone. He listened to the conversation for a moment before he realized that Ileana was talking to her mother Marie, the Queen of Romania.

"I'm just worried about you, that's all," Marie was saying.

Outside in the hall, Konstantin tensed up. *Is there a problem, this close to the wedding?* he wondered.

"You're only sixteen, a year younger than I was when I got married," Marie continued. "I thought I was too young. I can't believe I consented to let you marry even younger."

"It's different, Mama," Ileana said. "We've known Alyosha forever, and he's worried his hemophilia will cut his life short. We both know we wouldn't be marrying this early if it weren't for that."

There was a silence, and in the hallway, Konstantin strained his ears, wondering if the conversation was over. He raised his hand to knock on the door, and was about to bring his hand into contact with the door when Ileana started speaking again.

"Do you remember, Mama, all those years ago, when one of the Russian princes came asking for Elizabeth's hand in marriage?"

"How could I forget?" Marie asked, and she did not sound happy.

"Which one was it?" Ileana asked. "It was so long ago that I don't remember- I was so young that I didn't know of such things."

"It doesn't matter now, honey," Marie said. "Elizabeth is happily married in Greece."

"It matters to me, now that I know Alyosha's family better," Ileana said. "Was it Igor? You know he's Alyosha's ADC, and quite faithful to him."

"No, it wasn't Igor."

"Who, then? One of his brothers?"

"It was Konstantin," Marie said, with some hesitation.

"Oh, Konstantin," Ileana said. "But I like him immensely. Did you know he was decorated for fighting with bravery in the Great War? And his children are so adorable."

"Perhaps he and Pilar are a better match than he and Elizabeth would have been," Marie answered, but even out in the hall, Konstantin could hear the doubt in her voice.

There was another pause in the conversation, but Konstantin felt his courage slipping away. He was about to simply slip out of the palace when the silence in the room in front of him continued.

*I'm sure this is tough on Ileana*, Konstantin thought. *And she is the reason I came here in the first place.* He took a deep breath. *To hell with Marie*, he finally decided, and, curling up his hand into a ball, he knocked on the door in front of him. There was another silence in front of him, but after a minute the door opened, and Konstantin found himself looking at Marie. "Good evening, Marie," he said. "I came to offer my congratulations. I don't suppose Ileana is here?"

Marie looked at him for a moment, but then she stepped aside and turned to look at Ileana. Ileana looked up at Konstantin and smiled. Then she stood. "That parade the other day from the train station was magnificent," she said. "I caught a glimpse of you on horseback from my carriage, but I didn't have the chance to say anything."

Konstantin smiled in reply. "It was my honor to ride in it," he said. "A new tsarina, coming into St. Petersburg? We don't get to see that every day."

"Well, I'm not tsarina yet," Ileana said, her disarming smile remaining on her face.

"Wait a day or two," Konstantin said. Then he paused for a moment. "I hope it's not too overwhelming for you. I know our court and our customs can demand a lot, so I just wanted to say that you have my complete support." Konstantin felt his heart beating wildly in chest, and he kept his eyes on Ileana as he tried to ignore Marie's glower.

But Ileana continued to radiate warmth. "At least our religions are quite similar, and of course our families have known each other forever. That quite eases the transition."

"I do hope so," Konstantin said. *I really mean it.* "And if you need any help, you know where to find me and my family."

"I do indeed," Ileana replied.

Finally, Marie spoke from behind her daughter. "Did you come alone?" she asked Konstantin. "Where's Pilar?"

"She's in Bavaria, visiting her parents. Unfortunately, her mother was quite ill, but she is recovering. Pilar is on her way back already, and she'll be here in time for the wedding."

"I am looking forward to seeing her," Ileana said.

"The feeling is mutual," Konstantin replied. Then, with nothing else to say, he drew himself up to his full height and stood formally. "Well, it was good to see you both. Congratulations again, Ileana, and I'll see you at the wedding ceremony."

Ileana smiled in return. "You definitely will."

# THE DYNASTY CONTINUES

"Papa," Prince Sergei Konstantinovich said. "What did Ileana and Alyosha name the baby?"

"I don't know," Konstantin replied, smiling down at his six-year-old son as the carriage in which they were traveling rattled around them. "We're going to the christening so that we can learn what the baby's name will be."

For a minute, Sergei stared out the window as both Konstantin and Pilar smiled at him. "Papa," Sergei said again, looking back at Konstantin, "why didn't we bring Boris with us?"

"He's too little," Konstantin replied.

"But he's three years old already," Sergei said. "He's a big boy."

"Yes, he is," Konstantin solemnly agreed. "But we have to adhere to strict court protocol. Did you know that my brothers and I weren't allowed to attend court functions like this until we were much older than you?"

Sergei's mouth turned downwards into a frown. "I'll behave myself," he said. "And Boris would have too."

*Thick as thieves you two are,* Konstantin thought. He glanced over at Pilar, who was six months pregnant with their third child. *If we have another boy, we'll have a whole cadre of secret-*

*keeping children*, he thought. *Perhaps I should have thought of that sooner.*

The carriage stopped in front of the Winter Palace, and a footman in an elaborate outfit opened the door. Sergei grinned at the footman, who did his best to maintain a serious expression. "I like his outfit, Papa," Sergei giggled as they went into the Palace.

"Me too," Konstantin whispered conspiratorially.

Pilar eyed both of them. "Alyosha was worried about having children present as such a solemn occasion," she said. "Maybe he should have worried about some of the adults, too."

"I'll behave," Konstantin replied.

Inside the palace, the ceremony began and Princess Elizaveta Golitzina carried the baby down the aisle of the church on a white cushion. Konstantin strained his neck to see the baby, and saw a large, chubby infant on the pillow. *He looks large and healthy*, Konstantin thought. *Maybe the hemophilia that has plagued Alexei so will skip his son.*

As Princess Golitzina passed him, Konstantin glanced at Sergei, whom he was holding so that the boy could see better. Sergei was staring at the baby in front of him with wide eyes. His head turned as Princess Glitzina passed, and Konstantin could feel him straining to see more. Then Konstantin looked towards the front of the room, where the Dowager Empress Alexandra, who had been named as godmother, stood. Alexandra looked glowingly happy. *That may be the first time I've seen her smiling*, Konstantin thought.

The baby shrieked when the priest lifted him from the cushion, and he struggled when the priest immersed him in the font to baptize him. Water flew everywhere as the baby kicked his legs and wriggled his arms, and soon the priest's vestments were visibly wet. Konstantin cringed at the baby's distress, and was relieved when the baby started wailing again after being removed from the font.

Then the baby's name was pronounced, and the word "Konstantin" rang throughout the chapel.

Konstantin inhaled sharply, certain that his ears had deceived him. *They named the heir to the throne after me and Papa?* he thought. His mind was working so hard that it could barely form the words. His body felt transported, and for a minute, he was sure that his feet were not touching the ground. Only by pressing his toes more firmly into his boots could Konstantin be sure that gravity had not released him. He looked over at his family and saw that his mother and siblings were smiling.

"Tsar Konstantin," Ioann whispered.

Konstantin felt as though he could not move. It was only Sergei's squirming in his arms that brought him back to the present, and he finally noticed that the ceremony was over. Alexei and Ileana dashed into the chapel, and Konstantin and his siblings moved as one unit to surround them. "You named the Heir after Papa!" Konstantin exclaimed.

"I like it," Igor said, grinning.

"Our family will finally have a Tsar Konstantin," Ioann added.

"That's the hope," Alexei said as Ileana stood on her tiptoes, trying to locate the child.

It was only then that Konstantin realized that the young couple was likely worried about their baby, and he stepped aside to let Alexandra, who was holding the little Konstantin, come through and hand him to Ileana.

Once the baby was in sight, Sergei fixed his eyes on him again. "Look, Papa," he said. "The baby."

"I see him," Konstantin replied.

Vsevolod also stepped forward to get a better look at his newest cousin. When the baby's large eyes focused on him, he started making faces, trying to get little Konstantin to smile. His younger sister, Ekaterina, rolled her eyes and groaned at him. "Sevka was acting like that before the ceremony began, too," she said to Alexei.

Alexei looked amused as he reached for his son's hand, but Ioann was less forgiving about his oldest son's behavior. "Sevka is capable of behaving," he said as he crooked his arm around Vsevolod's neck.

Vsevolod stood up as straight as possible, and he looked worried as Ioann's arm only tightened further around his neck.

"Relax, Ioannchick," Konstantin said. "Sevka was only being silly."

"On what should be a solemn occasion," Ioann replied.

Then little Konstantin broke up the argument by smiling. Ioann, seeing the baby's wide grin, finally let go of his son, and Vsevolod shot little Konstantin a grateful smile.

Konstantin glanced back and forth between Vsevolod and the family's newest addition. *Those two are going to be friends for life,* he thought.

# LOSSES AND DESPAIR

The early morning ring of the telephone jangled Konstantin's nerves. *Who could that be?* he wondered. He headed for the still-foreign contraption, if only to make its noise stop. "Kostya, it's Igor," he heard his younger brother say a minute later.

"Is everything alright?" Konstantin asked. "It's unlike you to call this early." *Usually you have some level of consideration for when I don't have to train with my regiment and can sleep late. Though it's not that early. I really ought to cut him some slack.*

"I didn't mean to bother you," Igor said. "But Sophie is sick."

"What's the problem?"

"The doctors are still examining her, so I'm not sure yet, but I think it's about the baby."

Igor's voice shuddered, and Konstantin knew immediately that his brother was crying. "We'll be right over," he said. Within a few minutes, Konstantin and Pilar were being driven through the February snow to Igor's mansion on the Nevsky Prospect. Konstantin drummed his fingers on the car door. "I'm worried about this, Pilar," he told his wife. "Igor's doctors told him and Sophie not to have any more kids after

Oleg was born. They said it was such a difficult birth that there was a risk."

"And yet Igor has wanted a large family since before he got married," Pilar said, squinting as the clouds parted and sunlight poured into the car. "I'm not surprised that they tried for another."

Konstantin sighed as they went inside Igor's mansion. He didn't feel any better when he saw Igor, whose grim expression dashed his hopes for better news. "What's happening, Igor?" he asked.

"It's not good," Igor said, shaking his head. "There was a lot of blood. The doctors say she lost the baby."

"Oh my God," Pilar said, and Konstantin felt himself recoiling as well.

"I'm so sorry," Konstantin said as he went to embrace his brother.

"Where is Sophie?" Pilar asked.

"In our bedroom," Igor said. Tears fell from his eyes. "She doesn't want to see me."

Konstantin put his arm around Igor again and steered him towards one of the mansion's drawing rooms. Pilar waited just long enough for them to get inside before slipping off to see if Sophie would see her, at least. Konstantin sent a grateful look at his wife's back. *Thank God for her,* he thought. *Sophie shouldn't be alone now either.*

Igor collapsed into an armchair. "I never should have asked Sophie to have another child," he wept.

"This is not your fault," Konstantin replied.

"Yes, it is," Igor insisted. "I was the one who wanted more, even after the doctors told us it would be a risk."

Just then, Ioann and Elena slipped into the room, and Konstantin was glad for their presence, even if Igor sent them a slightly hostile look. "Take it easy, Igor," Konstantin advised. *It's not Ioann and Elena's fault they have six kids.*

By the time the phone rang later in the evening, Gavril, Maud, and George had come to Igor's home as well. The phone continued to ring, but Igor didn't seem inclined to answer it. *What if that's one of the doctors?* Konstantin wondered as he stood to answer the phone.

"Kostya, it's Alexei," the tsar said on the other end of the phone. "Is Sophie feeling any better?"

Konstantin glanced at Igor before answering, but Igor's blank countenance gave him no direction. "No, she lost the baby," he said into the phone. *I don't know what else to say,* he thought. *I can't lie.* So, he put Igor on the phone, but cringed as his brother stumbled through an explanation of the day's events.

"No, I don't think there's anything you can do," Igor told Alexei. "All of my brothers are here."

The next day, Konstantin and his siblings filled Igor's house again, and yet still Konstantin didn't see Sophie. "Is she feeling any better, at least?" he asked Igor.

"Not well enough to come down or deal with me," Igor said.

As the daytime turned into evening, Alexei and Ileana came over, and Konstantin wondered if their presence would finally pull Igor out of his sadness. Instead, Igor dissolved into tears. "I'm a bad person," he said. "Why else would this be happening to me?"

"That's not even remotely true," Gavril said, standing up and putting his hands on Igor's shoulders. "You are an exemplary person. What's happening now doesn't detract from that."

*I would agree,* Konstantin, but try as he might, he couldn't force the words out past the lump in his throat.

Peter and Nicholas crept into the room and crawled onto Igor's lap. Igor hugged his sons without reservation. "I should check on Oleg," he said of his youngest child.

"He's already asleep," Nicholas replied.

Konstantin eyed the three of them- his two small nephews in his tall brother's lap. *Hopefully the boys Igor already has will fill the void of the one he just lost,* he thought.

# ANOTHER HARD DAY

February 27, 1929
Strelna Palace
11:30 p.m.


God, what a day! Sleep has proven elusive, despite how early the winter's night descends on St. Petersburg. With the grace of God, perhaps some writing will alleviate my wakefulness.

Last night, Sophie fled back to Vienna under cover of that darkness, taking Oleg with her and leaving Igor with nothing but a note saying where she had gone. I know she is hurting from the loss of her pregnancy, but is fleeing with their child any way to treat her husband? And Oleg is barely out of infancy himself- now poor Igor is worried sick over both of them. Oleg is still their son, much as that lost child was, and a son needs his father present in his life. I hope this is just a passing episode, and that Sophie realizes that her selfishness affects her whole family.

Igor wants Oleg back as much as he wants Sophie back, and at least he is willing to go to Vienna to try to patch things up. Just this morning, Igor left Nicky and Petya at

Pavlovsk with Ioann and Elena. The boys will stay there as long as their parents are in Vienna.

I also offered to take Nicky and Petya- they would be as welcome here at Strelna as they are at Pavlovsk, but I think Igor preferred the idea of them staying at our childhood palace. Either way, they would be surrounded by a loving aunt and uncle, as well as a set of cousins around their age who will look after them.

I have to sympathize with Igor- this was not an easy decision. His first instinct was to give Sophie her space to work out her feelings, and hope that the distance between them would lead to a happy conclusion. If Sophie had fled to Vienna alone, Igor probably would have followed that path, but having Oleg taken away was too much for him to bear. It was Oleg's absence, and the hope that seeing Sophie again would resolve the situation more quickly, that sent Igor after his wife.

I do not envy him being in this situation, but I think he did the right thing. Petya and Nicky will be well cared for, and they will stay in Russia. With any luck, Igor will be returning to Russia with both Sophie and Oleg, and the family can move forward from these painful events. Both Sophie and Igor love all three boys, and Sophie would have to be blind not to see that Igor cares for her immensely as well.

These next few days will be long ones, and I await the conclusion of this sad affair with both hope and uncertainty.


Konstantin


Postscript- March 8, 1929: Igor, Sophie and Oleg have returned safely to St. Petersburg, thanks be to God. Igor is in a better mood now, and Sophie is improving. Even little Oleg seems happy, and it all gives me hope for the future.

# TOUGH COMMANDER

Prince Konstantin Konstantinovich slammed down his riding crop and stormed off the training field at Krasnoe Selo. One of the base's stable boys picked up the riding crop, but Konstantin, in his rage, barely noticed him. *Russia has already been through a huge war against Germany and half of Europe,* he thought. *If these regiments think they'll be able to defend Russia against another war of that magnitude, they're sadly mistaken! They can't shoot, and they can barely ride.*

Konstantin had to stop himself from yelling in frustration. *These are supposed to be the elite guards regiments, not simply enlisted men,* he thought. *It's wonderful that they're all tall and good-looking, and that their uniforms are perfect, but none of that is going to help them in wartime.*

Konstantin took a deep breath and felt the cool early autumn air reach his lungs. His mind continued working as he reached Krasnoe Selo's officers' club. *The Great War has only been over for thirteen years, and already people are forgetting its lessons,* he thought. *So many of our elite officers were unprepared for that war because they preferred parties and decorations over training.*

Inside the officers' club, Konstantin caught sight of his brothers Ioann and Gavril and made his way over to them. *They always stand out,* he thought. *I'm glad I'm tall, but I've never been as tall as they are, and actually, I can't complain. As an officer and a member of the imperial family, I'll always be a target in battle. If I were Ioann and Gavril's height, that would only make the enemy's job easier.*

Ioann and Gavril gave Konstantin a friendly nod as he joined them. Their smiles were as warm as ever, but still Konstantin could see something else in their eyes. "What?" he asked.

"Your face looks like a thundercloud," Gavril said. "Hopefully you didn't yell too much on your way over here."

"Me, yell?" Konstantin asked, even if that was exactly what he felt like doing. *Maybe my regiment would pay more attention if I did act like that.*

But Ioann was shaking his head. "We'll discuss it on our way back to Pavlovsk," he said.

"Who said we were going back to Pavlovsk?" Konstantin replied. "Pilar and the kids are at Strelna, and I intend to go straight there."

Ioann continued to eye Konstantin, and Konstantin finally got the message. *He's got something to say, he just doesn't want to say it here.*

"Fine," Konstantin said. "Pavlovsk it is."

It was not until the three brothers were being driven away from the officers' club that Gavril and Ioann eyed Konstantin again, and Konstantin could tell in that look alone that they were of one mind as to what they were about to say to him. Still, the car was silent for another minute as Gavril and Ioann decided what words to use. Konstantin took the extra time to examine the condensation that was gathering on the car's windows in the rapidly plunging autumn temperatures.

"Relax, Kostya," Gavril said finally. "You're too hard on your men."

"They have no discipline," Konstantin replied.

"You only think that because you saw how discipline frayed at the end of the Great War, and you want to avoid that," Ioann replied. "To a reasonable outsider, it doesn't look as bad as you think it does."

"There have been grumbles around officers' clubs- not just at Krasnoe Selo, but even around the city," Gavril said. "Both the officers and the enlisted men think you push too hard, past the point at which it encourages discipline."

"Really?" Konstantin asked. *I never intended to be that mean, but I can't forget the trench warfare of the Great War, either. That was brutal.*

"Your men like you, Kostya, and they admire both your bravery and your war record," Ioann said. "But you are too strict with them. If you continue on this path, you may lose the goodwill that they feel."

Konstantin took a deep breath and looked away as he contemplated the situation. When he looked back at Gavril and Ioann, they were still eyeing him seriously. "Perhaps you're right," he said. "The men are frustrated at how hard I'm working them. But the fact remains that many of them still need work in some of the basic soldiering skills."

"Then find a way to instill those qualities without making the men mutiny," Ioann said.

They had arrived at the Marble Palace, and Gavril put a hand on the car door with the intention of getting out. "We Romanovs will always be under an extra layer of scrutiny," he said. "Make sure we live up to people's expectations."

"I will," Konstantin said. Then he nodded at the Palace. "I saw your kids at the window when we first pulled up," he told Gavril. "Better get inside before they start running to us."

"Too late," Ioann said, laughing as he saw his niece and nephew opening the door to the palace and sprinting outside.

Gavril's son Nicholas was in the lead, and his daughter Anna was not far behind him. "Papa!" they yelled.

Gavril swept them up into his arms. "Kolya! Anya!" he said.

Konstantin and Ioann laughed as they hugged their niece and nephew. Then they got back in the car and headed on their way.

After spending nearly a week contemplating his brothers' advice, Konstantin began the day's training at Krasnoe Selo by having his men line up at attention before him. Then he spoke to them, choosing his words carefully as he paced back and forth in front of the assembled soldiers. "It has come to my attention that many of you are of the opinion that my training methods are too harsh. I have only implemented the current regimen because I recall what it was like in the trenches, fighting the Germans in the Great War. I can't imagine that we'll ever see another war of that magnitude, and yet Russia needs officers and soldiers who are prepared for any conflict.

"At the same time, bearing in mind the input I have received from other officers, I have decided that there is some merit to the argument that I am too severe. From this time forward, I will implement a slightly lesser training regime. However, should our standards slip as a regiment, and as an army, you can expect an increase in the discipline."

Konstantin paused before speaking again. "One last thing, men. It pains me that your frustration had to reach my ears from sources other than yourselves. I may be your commanding officer, but I do not intend to be a distant, unreachable figure. If you have any problems with the way I lead, tell me first, and I will do my best to address those problems."

Konstantin could feel sweat rolling down his back despite the weather's persistent coolness. He waited a minute to see whether his message was being received by the men in front of him. To his relief, the soldiers were nodding, and Konstantin could see what he thought was admiration in the eyes of many of them.

"Are there any questions?" Konstantin asked.

"No, sir!" the soldiers shouted.

"Good! Dismissed!"

The soldiers turned smartly and march back to the barracks. The sound of their boots hitting the ground echoed off the buildings around them. Konstantin watched as the men marched off. When the square was empty and silent, he smiled.

# BREAKING OUT OF MY SHELL

It was a bright spring day in 1932 when Konstantin, Pilar, Sergei, Boris and Olga walked into a restaurant in St. Petersburg to have lunch. The restaurant overlooked the Neva River, and the family was given a seat by the window. "Hooray!" Sergei cheered as he climbed into his chair. "I love looking out the window!" He pressed his face to the glass, and Boris, sitting across from him, followed suit.

Konstantin and Pilar smiled at each other as Pilar settled Olga on to her lap. Konstantin looked around the room, admiring the floor-to-ceiling windows that let in so much light. Sunlight swirled across the ceiling in the same pattern as the water in the Neva. As the family's soup was served, Konstantin caught sight of a stocky man sitting across the restaurant with his family. Keeping one eye on his soup, Konstantin watched as the man persuaded his young daughter to try a food of which she clearly was not fond.

"What are you looking at?" Pilar asked, unable to find the source of her husband's interest with a quick glance behind her.

"It's not a what, it's a who," Konstantin replied. "I think that gentleman at the table over there is Major Georgy Konstantinovich Zhukov."

"Who?" Sergei asked, pushing himself up onto his knees in his chair and staring across the room.

"Stop it," Konstantin hissed. He put down his soup spoon and maneuvered Sergei's legs out from under him until he was sitting normally.

"Who is he?" Pilar asked.

"He was a soldier who became a noncommissioned officer during the Great War. He was also decorated a few times over and has quite the reputation in the Army. Alyosha met him shortly after he became tsar and was impressed by him. He's become an officer since then. I've always wanted to meet him."

"You should go say hello," Boris said with a grin.

"I don't know," Konstantin said. "He's having lunch with his family. I'd hate to interrupt."

"Perhaps you ought to consider it anyway," Pilar advised her husband. "Getting out of your shell is never a bad thing. Besides, he may know your reputation as well as you know his."

Konstantin shrugged doubtfully as their soup bowls were cleared. Then he glanced over at Sergei and Boris and found that they were watching him. *I'd hate to have them inherit my shyness,* he thought. He looked back over to where Zhukov was sitting and saw that the family's dishes had already been cleared, and that they were simply sitting and talking. "Perhaps you're right," he said to Pilar. "I will go introduce myself."

As he stood and made his way over to where Zhukov was sitting, Konstantin felt many eyes on him. *I'll bet anything Pilar is right,* he thought. *These people know who I am.*

He took a deep breath as he neared Zhukov's table. When Zhukov looked up at him, he nodded and smiled. "Are you Major Zhukov?" he asked.

"I am," he said.

"I am Konstantin Konstantinovich Romanov, a colonel in the Izmailovsky Regiment."

Zhukov smiled, and Konstantin almost felt himself relaxing. "Your reputation precedes you, of course," Zhukov said.

"As does yours," Konstantin replied. "I just wanted to introduce myself. I didn't want to be a stranger to a man of your caliber."

Zhukov almost looked embarrassed. "Your Serene Highness is too kind," he said.

*So he does know who I am*, Konstantin thought. *I never said I was a prince.*

Zhukov introduced his family, and Konstantin smiled at them. "Highness?" Zhukov's daughter Era asked.

"It means he's a member of the Imperial family," Zhukov told her.

"Imperial, like the tsar?" Era asked.

"Yes, the tsar is my cousin," Konstantin said.

"Wow," Era said. "I've always wanted to meet the tsar."

"I met him years ago, right after he became tsar," Zhukov told her.

"I know," Era said with a shy smile as she looked back at Konstantin.

"I think I've seen your brother here more often than you," Zhukov said to Konstantin. "Prince Gavril."

"Yes, that would make sense," Konstantin said. "He likes this place a lot." *And he's much more social than I am.*

"Is Prince Gavril the really tall one?" Era asked her father.

"Yes," Konstantin answered her, laughing as he spoke. His humor seemed to put the Zhukovs at ease. Then glanced back at his own family and realized that they were being served their main course. He looked back at Zhukov. "Well, don't let me disturb your lunch any further."

"You weren't, Your Serene Highness," Zhukov replied.

"Please don't hesitate to call on me for anything," Konstantin said.

"I won't," Zhukov promised.

Konstantin gave them one last nod and made his way back to his table, where Pilar and his kids were waiting for him before eating their main course.

"Now, was that so bad?" Pilar teased her husband.

"It could have been worse," Konstantin admitted as he watched Zhukov and his family leave the restaurant out of the corner of his eye.

"Did he know who you were, Papa?" Sergei asked.

"Yes, he did. He also said he's seen Gavril in here on a number of occasions."

"See, I told you he'd be familiar with the family," Pilar said as she fed Olga. "Aren't you glad you said something to him?"

Konstantin nodded seriously as he took a bite of his fish. "Yes, I am," he said. "I think we'll see more of Zhukov in the future."

# UNEXPECTED VISITORS

Konstantin sat in his study in his family's palace of Strelna, enjoying the rare quiet. *The children are still in their lessons, and Pilar is having lunch downtown with Elena and Ileana,* he thought as the early afternoon light streamed into the study. *I've gotten more done since I started working this morning than in the past several days combined. I could get used to this.*

Suddenly, a loud squeal ended the silence. Konstantin jumped. *What on Earth was that?* he wondered. *It didn't sound like one of the children.*

Another squeal sounded, and this time, Konstantin also heard a couple of giggles from the hallway outside his study. *Perhaps the children are up to something after all,* he thought as he stood. Then he looked around his study, trying to locate the source of the squeals. *It sounds like it's coming from under that couch over there,* he thought as he made his way over to his favorite piece of furniture.

Sure enough, another screech emanated from under the couch. Konstantin knelt beside the couch and looked underneath it. A ball of fur with two tiny eyes stared back at him. "Hello," Konstantin said to the little kitten in front of him. "How did you get in here?"

There was another set of giggles from outside his study, and Konstantin had the feeling that was the answer to his question.

"Come here," he said to the kitten, and reached under the couch to pull it out. The kitten, scared, backed away from him, but Konstantin moved faster, and soon, he was holding a gray and white kitten with long fur. "Aaww," Konstantin said as he stood up again. "You look barely old enough to be away from your mama."

"Mikhail Ivanovich said he was already weaned," Konstantin heard someone say of the veterinarian who tended to the family's horses. He looked over to see his oldest son, Sergei, standing in the hallway, just outside the door to his study.

"I was wondering how he got in here," Konstantin said.

Sergei ducked and laughed, and Konstantin could see his younger son, Boris, behind Sergei, standing on his tiptoes, trying to see the kitten.

"Where has he been until now?" Konstantin asked.

"In the barn," Sergei said. "The mother snuck in there to have the little ones."

"And Mikhail Ivanovich has been caring for the mother and the kittens all this time?" Konstantin asked.

Sergei nodded. He came into his father's study and held out his hands for the kitten.

Konstantin handed it to him. "Be gentle," he ordered.

"I know," Sergei said. He grinned when he was holding the little animal. He started petting it, and soon Boris crept into the room to pet it too.

In a second, Konstantin could hear the kitten purring. Sergei and Boris grinned widely, and Konstantin's heart melted faster than the ice cream his sons had left in their rooms the day before. "How many kittens are there?" he asked.

Boris held up all five fingers on one hand.

"Five?" Konstantin said. "That's a lot. You can't keep all of them."

"I just want this one," Sergei said as he hugged the kitten to his chest.

Boris nodded in agreement. "He's the furriest and the cutest."

Konstantin eyed them for a minute. "Fine," he said. "I'll allow you to keep this one, as long as you help Mikhail Ivanovich to find homes for the other four."

Sergei and Boris looked at each other, then back at Konstantin. "How are we supposed to do that?" Boris asked.

"The how is up to you," Konstantin said, and watched for his sons' reaction.

Sergei and Boris looked at each other again. "I think we can find homes for them," Sergei said. "All of our tutors have children who might want kittens."

"Or they may have friends who'd want them," Boris said.

Konstantin nodded. "See?" he said. "I knew you'd come up with a solution."

# DEATH COMES A-KNOCKING

A sudden gust of wind threatened to knock Konstantin over as he stepped out of his motor car at Pavlovsk. For a brief moment, Konstantin looked upwards. His gaze travelled past yellow façade of his childhood palace and up to the sky. As the wind continued to bite into his skin, Konstantin expected to see at least a snowflake or two coming towards him. However, the sky, while threateningly overcast, seemed intent upon keeping its snowflakes to itself.

*It's only the second week in October,* Konstantin reminded himself as he was led inside. *We'll definitely get snow soon.*

"Uncle Kostya!" he heard someone call, and he turned to see Vsevolod, his oldest nephew, pushing his dark hair out of his face as he approached.

"Sevka," Konstantin said with a grin as they embraced. *He looks more like Elena and Alexander every day,* Konstantin thought of Vsevolod's mother and uncle.

Then Konstantin's brother Ioann, tall and blond, appeared behind his son. "Ready for lunch?" he asked.

"Absolutely," Konstantin said. They headed for the dining room, and Konstantin felt a twinge of nostalgia as he looked around. *Some of my fondest memories are of growing up in this palace,* he thought. *I'm almost jealous that Papa left it to Ioann.*

In the dining room, Elena and her three daughters, Ekaterina, Elizaveta, and Kira, were talking as they gathered around the table. Elena hugged Ioann and smiled at Konstantin. "How is Krasnoe Selo?" she asked. "Still busy with your regiment?"

"Always am," Konstantin said.

Vsevolod grinned. "I'm glad I finally started training in my regiment too," he said.

There was a clatter in the hallway, and Vsevolod's brothers, Vyacheslav and Gleb, raced into the room. "We want to start training with our regiments too!" they shrieked in unison.

Konstantin laughed. "Maybe you should enjoy being children first!" he said. *Vsevolod is definitely a man already, but he turned twenty this year. Vyacheslav and Gleb are only twelve and ten.*

Ioann eyed his youngest sons uneasily. "You'll start when you're old enough, and not a day before," he said. He looked back at Konstantin. "The Great War may have ended sixteen years ago, but I certainly haven't forgotten it. I'm not eager to have my sons train for war."

"Relax, Ioann, the military is what we Romanovs do," Konstantin replied as the family sat down at the table. "Besides, I doubt there will be another war of that magnitude-Alyosha is certainly doing his best to prevent one."

Ioann sighed as he thought of their cousin, Tsar Alexei II. "And yet still he and Ileana have gone to France to negotiate a political alliance," he said as their soup was served.

"In the hopes of preventing another war," Vsevolod said. "And at least he gets to see Uncle Sandro again."

"That's always nice," Elena agreed. She looked at Ioann. "I've been thinking of visiting Belgrade again soon if you want to come. I haven't seen Sandro in awhile either. He's too busy ruling over Yugoslavia to travel much."

"I'll go with you if you do," Vsevolod said. "Sandro's always been my favorite uncle. Aside from Kostya, that is." He and Konstantin shared a grin.

"You should definitely go," Ioann said. He thought for a moment as he looked back at Elena. "Your brother has done a lot as king. I've always been impressed by him."

Elena nodded. "I remember when we were just little Serbia. Things are so different now." She was about to say something else when the phone rang.

Everyone looked at each other, and it was Elena who put her spoon down, placed her napkin on the table, and went into the next room to answer the phone. "Hello, Alyosha," she said into the phone a minute later.

Konstantin, Vsevolod, and Ioann exchanged amused glances. "Alyosha must have heard us talking about him," Konstantin joked.

The words were barely out of his mouth when Elena's scream echoed through the palace. The family jumped, startled. Ioann dashed into the next room in the time it took his brother and children to push back their chairs and stand up. By the time Konstantin made it to the next room over, his nieces and nephews on his heels, Ioann was holding the phone to his left ear. His right arm was around Elena's shoulders as Elena sobbed.

"Are you sure about this, Alyosha?" Ioann asked.

"I was there, Ioannchick," Konstantin heard Alexei say through the phone. "He's dead."

"What?" Konstantin yelped, as he felt his heard begin to race. "What happened?"

Ioann held a hand up for Konstantin to be quiet. Then he spoke into the phone again. "Where are you now, Alyosha?" he asked. "Where is Igor?"

"Igor's fine," Alexei replied, and Konstantin felt some relief about his younger brother's safety. "We're both back at our hotel."

"Let us know when you know anything further," Ioann ordered before he hung up. Then he hugged Elena to his chest as he looked at Konstantin. "Alexei was calling from Marseilles," he said. "Alexander has been murdered."

"What?!" Konstantin and Vsevolod yelled at the same time. Konstantin felt his heart rate spike, and his face turned warm and red.

"How could that happen?" Vsevolod shrieked. "Wasn't there any police protection?"

"Not enough, apparently," Ioann answered.

Without warning, Vsevolod swung his fist into a nearby chair, and a loud crack followed as the chair split into two. Ioann let go of Elena and grabbed Vsevolod's hands as his younger children surrounded Elena. "Sevka," Ioann said. "You can't take your anger out on the furniture."

Vsevolod jerked away from his father. "How then?" he spat. "By going to war?"

Konstantin felt his head turning mechanically from side to side. "I hope we're not headed for another war."

Vsevolod glared at him. "Why not?" he asked. "Didn't the murder of an heir to the throne start the Great War? Why shouldn't the murder of a king start the next one?" He stormed out of the room.

Konstantin and Ioann stared at each other. Konstantin felt like his eyes were staring through Ioann's eyes and into his pained soul. His feet felt as though they were bolted to the floor. For a few seconds, nothing moved.

Then Ioann swallowed and looked away, towards the direction in which Vsevolod had fled. "I'm going after him," he said. "To make sure he doesn't do anything stupid."

"I should get back to Strelna," Konstantin agreed, even though his legs felt like lead, and he was having trouble moving towards the door. The sounds of Elena's continued sobs finally reached his ears. "I have to tell Pilar and my children. We should all travel to Belgrade together for the funeral."


It was on the train to Belgrade that Konstantin finally wept. Pilar took his hand as their daughter Marie sat on her lap. "I'm really sorry," she said. "This is such a stunning turn of events."

"I know," Konstantin said. "I can barely believe he's dead." He looked over to where Ioann was comforting Elena. Vyacheslav and Gleb sat with Vsevolod at a nearby table, talking quietly. Vsevolod's jaw was set and tense, and his eyes remained red.

Konstantin looked back at Pilar. "I'm just so relieved that Alyosha is unharmed," he said.

Pilar nodded. "Thanks in part to Igor, I heard."

"Yes, Alyosha said Igor helped him get out of there quickly."

"Igor's a brave man, Kostya. Alyosha's lucky to have him as an ADC."

Konstantin nodded and looked out the train window to the scenery just beyond it. *I'm worried about Olga, though,* he thought of Alexei's oldest sister. *Watching your husband get murdered in front of you may not be something you recover from.*

In Belgrade, Konstantin embraced Igor as soon as he saw him. Igor looked relieved to have his siblings there, but his eyes also carried a haunted look that scared Konstantin.

"Sophie and our boys arrived this morning," Igor said. "I'm so glad they weren't here when it happened."

Konstantin nodded. "Alexei and Ileana were thinking of bringing their kids too, as I recall," he said.

Igor shook his head. "They're just as glad they didn't, too." All of a sudden, tears fell from his eyes, and Konstantin pulled him back into a hug.

"Where is Alyosha?" Ioann asked as Konstantin released their younger brother.

"At our hotel," Igor replied.

"What about Olga?" Konstantin asked.

"She's back at the Palace with her children," Igor said. "Sandro's cousin Paul is over there now too."

"What the hell happened, Igor?" Vsevolod demanded as the family went into the hotel.

The rest of the family also turned to Igor for an answer, and Konstantin found himself straining to make sure he heard Igor's answer.

Igor sighed. "We were driving down the street in a procession of open cars," he began.

"An open car?" Vsevolod demanded as they headed towards their rooms. "Are you out of your mind?" Ioann put his arm around his son, but Vsevolod shook it off. Next to Vsevolod, Elena's tears continued flowing.

"It didn't seem stupid at time," Igor mumbled. "There were people lining the streets, cheering for both Sandro and Alyosha- 'long live the King! Long live the Tsar!'" He shook his head, and tears fell from his eyes again.

Once more, Konstantin put his arm around Igor, and this time, George stood at Igor's other side.

"I'm sorry," Vsevolod said as Igor sent a pained look in his direction. "I'm glad you and Alyosha are unharmed."

"Please don't do anything rash, Sevka," Igor said. "I think that all of us that were there are still in shock."

After the family had gotten settled in the hotel, Konstantin and Pilar left their children with Gavril and Maud and went to visit Olga. "I don't know what to expect, Pilar," Konstantin admitted as they drove to the palace.

Pilar nodded in agreement. "I'm almost counting on her being in bad shape."

At the Royal Palace, they were led inside, where Olga was sitting in one of the drawing room. She rose slowly when Konstantin and Pilar arrived, and her vacant stare scared Konstantin.

"Olga, I'm so sorry," Konstantin said. *I also have no idea what else to say,* he thought. *There are just no words for this.*

"I'm glad you could come," Olga said as Konstantin and Pilar embraced her. When they sat, Pilar sat next to Olga on the couch and took her hand. "I just don't know what to do now," Olga said.

"You shouldn't be deciding anything now," Pilar said.

"Would you want to come to Russia for a little while?" Konstantin asked. His childhood memories of Olga were very strong in his mind.

Olga's eyes moved towards him, but her gaze remained unfocused. "That's not a bad idea," she said. "I mean, it'll depend on what's happening here- Peter is too young to rule- there will need to be a Regency." She leapt to her feet and started pacing around the room. "Do you think I should be Regent?"

"I think you should discuss it with the family, and see what documentation Sandro may have left behind," Konstantin replied, choosing his words carefully. *She really shouldn't be rushing into anything.*

Slowly, Olga nodded. "That's a good idea," she said.

More than half a million people clogged the streets of Belgrade to mourn their king during the funeral procession, and Konstantin quickly felt claustrophobic. His tears streamed down his face, but his body still felt numb. *I can't believe this is happening,* he thought. He looked around him, and felt like his chest was being ripped open by the tears he saw all around him. Both Elena and Vsevolod were bawling, and Ioann had an arm around each of them, even as his own eyes remained red.

Further away, Igor was leaning on Sophie, and Konstantin became concerned for this brother of his that had witnessed the murder. *Where's Alyosha?* he wondered. He looked around, and saw that Alexei was alternating glances between the coffin in front of him and his oldest sister. *Olga still looks like a mannequin,* Konstantin thought, once again noticing Olga's stiff movements and vacant gaze. Throughout it all, Konstantin made sure to keep his arm around Pilar and his own children. *This isn't anything children should have to witness,* he thought.

By the time the funeral was over, Konstantin felt as

though all feeling and energy had been drained from his body. When Alexei and Ileana went to Ioann and Elena's hotel room, Konstantin forced his limbs to move so that he and Pilar could join them. The bags under Alexei's eyes conveyed his exhaustion. *I'm sure he's looking forward to going home,* Konstantin thought. *This can't be any easier on him than it has been on me.*

"Alyosha, I'm worried about Olga," Konstantin heard himself saying. "Maybe she should come back to Russia for a little while?"

"I thought of that," Alexei replied. "I'm sure it will depend on what's happening here with Peter's regency, but I'll make sure she knows that spending time in Russia is an option."

As their train pulled out of the station in Belgrade two days later, Konstantin was glad that Pilar was sitting next to him. Her presence alone comforted him, and yet a feeling of despair washed over him as the train picked up speed.

"What are you thinking, Kostya?" Pilar asked.

Konstantin shook his head as he looked back at her. "A king was just murdered in broad daylight in front of his wife and brother-in-law," he said. "What kind of world do we live in?"

# ENDINGS AND OPPORTUNITIES

The barracks at Krasnoe Selo were alive with shouts and gossip. Prince Konstantin Konstantinovich stood aghast, listening to the radio in front of him. "Don't look so upset, sir," said a young lieutenant in his regiment, Ivan Kuznetsov.

"The Japanese just invaded China, Ivan," Konstantin replied. "This means another war."

"Not on Russian soil, though," Ivan replied with a grin.

"Even so, I can't imagine we would simply stand by and watch," Konstantin replied, staring outside the barracks to where the summer sun was baking the ground. He took a deep breath and smelled both freshly-cut grass and the humid air of July, 1937, flowing through an open window.

Next to him, Ivan was still smiling as he listened to the news flowing from the radio. He shrugged when he saw Konstantin look back at him. "If it's contained to Japan and China, I can't imagine we Russians would bother," he said.

Konstantin shook his head. "I think nothing could be farther from the truth." *These young guys just don't get it,* he thought. *Russia sent troops to Japan in 1904 because we wanted to flex our military might, and that was a disaster. We're better prepared to fight now, and we have real interests in that area. I think our involvement is a distinct possibility.*

Then a messenger appeared at Konstantin's elbow. "Your Serene Highness, the Tsar is on the phone for you," he said.

Konstantin shot one last glance at Ivan before hurrying away. "Alyosha," he said into the phone a minute later. "This is a surprise."

"I'm sure it is," Alexei replied with a sigh. "But no more of a surprise than Japan's recent actions, I'm afraid."

"I just heard about that on the news," Konstantin said. "We're headed for another war, aren't we?"

Alexei sighed again. "That's what I'm hoping to talk to you about, Kostya," he said. "How soon can you make it to the Winter Palace?"

"We just finished our maneuvers for the day," Konstantin replied. "I'll be right over." He headed outside into the shimmering heat and blowing dust. *So this means war,* he thought, his stomach clenching. *I wonder where I'll be posted? I guess Japan, or China.* When he arrived at the Palace, he was ushered into Alexei's study and found Igor and Alexei alone there. "Igor," he said, smiling as he embraced his brother. "It's always good to see you."

A few minutes later, Colonel Georgy Konstantinovich Zhukov arrived, and Konstantin realized that Alexei had sent for both of them. The two colonels smiled at each other as they seated themselves across from Alexei and Igor. *I'm so glad I introduced myself to him all that time ago,* Konstantin thought as he remembered their first encounter in a restaurant on the Neva-a meeting that had been followed by parties and other get-togethers. *If we couldn't work together now, it would really be a problem.*

Across the desk, Alexei was eying Konstantin and Zhukov unhappily. "The Japanese attacks on the Chinese have really thrown a wrench into my desire to maintain peace, and they pose a threat to Russian interests in Vladivostok," he said.

"Are you thinking of sending in our Army, Your Imperial Majesty?" Zhukov asked, his eyes gleaming at the opportunity.

Alexei nodded. "I don't want this war to end in a rout like the war in 1904 did," he said. "At the same time, we've spent the last twenty years recovering from and moving forward from the Great War. If Hitler continues on his current path, we may well be headed for another war across Europe, and protecting our interests against Japan will at least give us the sense of how prepared we are."

Konstantin swallowed and felt how dry his throat was. *I really want this,* he thought. *If I lead our armies to victory here, I may get that long-awaited promotion to general.* "Send me anywhere," he said, looking Alexei directly in the eye. "I'm happy to lead."

Both Alexei and Igor smiled at him. "That's what I was hoping to hear," Alexei said. "Kostya, I'm putting you in charge of the 38th Corps. Colonel Zhukov, I'm putting you in charge of the 57th Corps. Prepare to march out as soon as possible."

As soon as he was out of the Winter Palace, Konstantin rushed back to Krasnoe Selo, and then to Strelna to prepare for the mobilization. At Strelna, Pilar watched him with tears in her eyes. "Another war," she said.

"A small one," Konstantin replied. *I don't want to minimize this action, but I don't want to worry her either.*

"The last time Russia said that about a war against Japan, it lost," Pilar reminded her husband.

"I'm well aware," Konstantin replied as he laid his rifle and cleaning materials out on a table. Sergei, Boris, Olga and Marie appeared behind Pilar, and Konstantin eyed his sons in particular. *If this war fails, or if Hitler keeps marching across Europe, they'll be fighting too. It's worth my death in this "little war" against Japan to prevent that.*

Two months later, Konstantin and Zhukov were leading their armies against the Japanese along the banks of the Khalkhin-Gol River. The Chinese army had been outfitted with Russian guns and tanks, and the Russians had done their best to train their Chinese allies in modern warfare. *That training would have gone farther if it hadn't been under fire from the Japanese,* Konstantin thought as bullets whizzed by his ear.

The land around the river was completely flat, and the lack of cover exposed the troops on both sides. The Russian air force had taken to bombing the Japanese, but the Japanese air force was responding with equal ferocity. Konstantin could hear the planes whining overhead, and he looked up to see Russian bombs being dropped.

The bombs hit their targets, and yet Konstantin's stomach still dropped. *Sergei's been in love with planes ever since he was little, and he's spent his entire military time in Russia's air force,* he thought. *Those skills will send him to the front lines, not protect him. We need to end this war, and not start another.*

When the fall turned into winter, snow poured out of the sky, and it made Konstantin long for the fresh snow falling on St. Petersburg. He shook his hat out as he stepped into their headquarters to confer with Colonel Zhukov, sending snowflakes everywhere as he did. Then he looked at Zhukov to find him smiling.

"This war is nearly over, Kostya," Zhukov said.

Konstantin nodded. "My army has covered over thirty kilometers today alone, chasing the Japanese back."

"And my intelligence officers have just reported back, saying that the Japanese's supply lines are running low, and that there is talk of a final retreat."

"I have always admired your emphasis on reconnaissance and intelligence," Konstantin replied. "I think it has gone a long way in this war."

Zhukov continued to smile as he stood. "Let's hope it helps end this war," he said. "Now, tell me about that offensive you were thinking of launching."

When the new year came, it was obvious that the war was nearly over, but Konstantin was more lonely than relieved. *1938*, he thought. *I never would have guessed that I would be spending another holiday season away from my family.* During a break in the fighting, Konstantin called his men together for a toast. "To the New Year," he said. "To winning this war and getting home." *To my promotion to general.*

The soldiers raised their flasks and shot glasses and cheered. Everyone drank.

*It still feels like a solemn occasion,* Konstantin thought. *None of these men really want to be away from their families. Besides, we've lost so many soldiers in the fighting that each of the men here knows someone who's no longer with us.*

At the end of January, Konstantin lifted his binoculars to his eyes to survey the Japanese position. Then he frowned, his eyebrows knitting together in uncertainty. *If it weren't snowing again, I would almost think those are white flags,* he thought, feeling his heart rate increasing. *Are the Japanese surrendering?* He lowered his binoculars and went to find Zhukov. Together the two colonels surveyed the white flags in front of them. "Let's send out a small party to see if they're serious," Konstantin said.

"They'd better be," Zhukov said. "They don't have an army left."

When a full peace had been negotiated, the Russian army went home like heroes. Konstantin grinned as they arrived back in St. Petersburg. *It's nearly springtime,* he thought as the train pulled into the capital on a sunny day in early March. Pilar wrapped her arms around her husband. "I'm so glad you're home safely," she said as their children surrounded them.

"Me too," Konstantin replied, still feeling the rocking of the train, even as he stood on solid ground with snow beneath his boots.

The next day brought a telegram that Konstantin had spent the last couple of months praying for. Dashing into the formal dining room where his family was just gathering to have supper, Konstantin held up the telegram and grinned, feeling the dry paper in between his fingers. "From Alexei," he said. "My promotion to general."

Sergei and Boris whooped in unison, drowning out the rest of the family's reactions. In a second, though, Olga and Marie had joined their brothers' cheers. Pilar shot them all a look that said that she would have thrown a sharp object in their direction if she thought it prudent. "Congratulations," she told her husband.

"Thank you," Konstantin replied, feeling as though his grin would split his face apart.

Later that night, after he had spoken to Alexei and expressed his sincere thanks, Konstantin sat in front of the fire in one of the palace's drawing rooms. Once more, he felt the dry telegram between his fingers as he felt the warmth of the fire on his knees. The fire crackled, and Konstantin jumped, thinking of the planes that had been flying above him only a few months before.

Suddenly realizing how fast his heart was racing, Konstantin took a deep breath and resettled himself into his chair. He was just wishing he had his flask with him when his family surrounded him. Sergei and Boris were grinning, and Pilar, Olga and Marie were smiling too.

"Congratulations, Papa," Boris said, holding out a shot glass.

Konstantin looked at him and realized that he was carrying a set of shot glasses and a decanter on a silver tray. He took the glass that his son was offering and watched as Boris distributed the rest of the glasses to his siblings and mother. As Boris unscrewed the decanter, Konstantin felt the chill of the glass he held, and took a closer look at it. Gold trim surrounded the outside of the lid, and the Romanov double-headed eagle was embossed on it. "Where did you get these?" Konstantin asked as he realized that the glasses and decanter were all part of a matching set.

"From the Obolenskys' glass factory outside of Moscow," Boris replied with a grin as he filled Konstantin's glass with vodka from the decanter. "When your armies won the war against Japan, I ordered this to celebrate."

"And with your promotion to general, I thought it even more appropriate," Pilar said, raising her glass.

"This is Zhukov's victory as well, don't forget," Konstantin replied after he emptied his glass. "He's an incredible leader, and he's bring promoted to general as well."

Sergei smiled at his father as Boris refilled their glasses. "I still haven't forgotten the time you were trying to decide whether to introduce yourself to him in that restaurant."

Konstantin laughed. "I was remembering that myself recently."

The promotion ceremony was held in late March in the Concert Hall of the Winter Palace. When Konstantin arrived with his family in tow, he found that Zhukov had already arrived with his wife and daughters. "Congratulations, Georgy Konstantinovich," he said.

"The same to you," Zhukov replied with a smile. "You are as deserving of this as I am."

When the ceremony began, Konstantin stood stiffly at attention as Alexei pinned the decoration on his chest. He clenched his facial muscles to make sure that he did not grin like an idiot. *This is a solemn occasion, Kostya,* he reminded himself. Still, he felt his pride beating within him like a drum, and his eyes felt like they were sparkling. "Thank you, Your Imperial Majesty," Konstantin said when Alexei had finished pinning the decoration on his chest.

"You are very welcome," Alexei replied. "You continued service to this country has been more than honorable."

Konstantin watched as Alexei moved over to Zhukov, and he suddenly noticed the authority that Alexei projected. *I've spent most of my life thinking of Alyosha as a child,* he thought. *Part of that is the thirteen year age gap between us, but part of it is the fact that he took the throne at sixteen, when he still was a child in many respects.*

When the ceremony was over, Konstantin and Pilar wrapped their arms around each other. Then Konstantin hugged Sergei, Boris, Olga and Marie as his siblings and their families surrounded him.

"I'm very proud of you, Kostya," Ioann said.

"Congratulations," Gavril added as he clapped Konstantin on the shoulder.

"Thank you," Konstantin replied, noticing that his large extended family took up most of the room. As he watched, however, his nephew Nicholas broke away from the group and went to talk to Zhukov.

"Nicky's been training with the big guns, and he loves it," Igor said as he watched his second son congratulate Zhukov. "He served under Zhukov for awhile before you both went to China."

"I remember that," Konstantin replied. "I hear he's quite the shot."

Igor nodded. "The imperial family's first sniper," he said.

Konstantin shuddered as he pictured his nephew on rooftops, killing unsuspecting people. "Let's hope we never have to use those skills," he said. "War is a horror."

# THE CLOUDS OF WAR

Konstantin grinned at his youngest brother, George, as they finished the tour of George's mansion in St. Petersburg. "I love what you've done to this place," he said. Next to him, Pilar nodded, and George's wife Grace smiled as well.

"We were really trying to decide what we wanted in an urban home," Grace said. "Buying this place, and then renovating it, has been a process."

"A long, drawn-out process," George admitted.

"With great results, though," Pilar said. "Every piece of your wood furniture is fabulous. I absolutely love it."

George's grin lit up his face. "We've been specializing in that for some time," he said. "We get a lot of wood from American forests, but the birch wood we use is exclusively Russian."

"Your wood factory outside the city is quite well known now," Konstantin said. "I've always been impressed by the products it makes."

"So much so that he's almost let me buy some of its furniture for Strelna," Pilar quipped.

George and Grace laughed.

"After seeing the furniture you have here, I may finally order some," Konstantin said seriously as they all went into George's study. "It is quite nice."

Outside, the winter sun was approaching the horizon, sending long rays of light across the sky. *The sun has barely even been above the horizon at all today, and yet it's already nearly nighttime,* Konstantin thought.

George turned on a lamp to illuminate his darkening study, then turned on the radio that sat on his desk. "I'm hoping for some news from Alyosha's visit with Hitler," he said. He looked over at Pilar. "Did you know they're meeting in Bavaria?"

Pilar nodded at the mention of her birthplace, but her eyes were sad. "Bavaria was my home until I came to St. Petersburg," she said. "And yet still I'm not sure I'd recognize it today. The Nazis have coopted it as their vacation spot. I can't say I approve."

George nodded in agreement. "We're all hoping that Alyosha's meeting will avert a war, but I wish I were more confident."

"Me too," Konstantin admitted. "I also expected that we'd hear from Igor when they were on their way home, but I haven't heard anything."

"We haven't either," Grace said.

"Should we call Sophie?" Pilar asked. "Maybe she's heard from him."

Konstantin and George looked at each other, doubtful looks on their faces. Then Konstantin shrugged. "I don't know that it's worth that much of an effort right now," he said. "I'm sure we'll hear from Alyosha at some point."

They were all silent as the radio in front of them began broadcasting the news. The broadcaster came back on, sounding like he was out of breath. Konstantin and George eyed each other, wondering what was coming. "The latest news here is that Alexei Nikolaievich, the Russian Tsar, has been killed following a meeting with German Chancellor Adolph Hitler," the broadcaster said.

"What!?" Konstantin and George shrieked in tandem. Next to them, Pilar and Grace gasped. "Shit!" Konstantin howled, feeling the blood drain from his face. "I can't believe this!"

George had turned as white as the paper on his desk. For a second, he gestured for silence so that they could hear the rest of the news broadcast. It was only with difficulty that Konstantin obeyed his brother- his heart was racing and sweat suddenly felt like it was pouring out of his body.

"Our sources tell us that the assassination occurred following a meeting regarding European peace that must have been anything but peaceful," the newscaster said. "Chancellor Hitler is already telling the German media that the Tsar threatened him during the meeting, and that one of his guards was only defending him when the Tsar was killed."

"No way!" Konstantin yelled.

George, too, was shaking his head. "The Germans must be lying," he said. "Alyosha would not have threatened Hitler to his face."

The news broadcast ended, and Konstantin, George, Pilar and Grace all stared at each other for a minute, their eyes wide with horror. "Time to call Sophie," Konstantin decided. "Maybe she's heard from Igor." *Igor was with Alyosha when this happened. There's no way he would have let Hitler kill him. None of this makes sense.*

George was already on the phone. "Have you heard anything?" he asked when Sophie answered.

"Ioann just called too," Sophie replied, and she sounded strangely calm.

*She must know something,* Konstantin thought. *She wouldn't be so composed otherwise.*

"Igor called a little while ago," Sophie continued. "The newscast must have gotten the wrong information. Hitler tried to kill Alyosha, but he didn't succeed. Igor said he and Alyosha's family had been travelling all night to get out of there as fast as possible. They should be back at the Winter

Palace by now." She took a deep breath. "I was about to head over there when you called."

"We're going too," Konstantin yelped, running for the door.

George nodded at him. "We'll meet you over there, Sophie," he said into the phone.

The high speed dash for the Winter Palace did little to calm Konstantin's nerves. As soon as their car came to a stop, he leapt out and sprinted for the palace doors. George, Pilar and Grace were on his heels. "Alyosha! Igor!" Konstantin yelled as soon as they were inside.

Vsevolod appeared in the hallway outside Alexei's study, and Ioann stood in the doorway behind him. Ioann jerked his head towards the study, and Konstantin raced towards him. Vsevolod and Ioann went back into the study, and Konstantin, Pilar, George and Grace followed. Inside, Konstantin saw Alexei, Ileana and all of their children. Their daughter Anastasia was crying, and their sons looked like they were about to join her. Ileana's eyes were also red.

Konstantin looked around for Igor, and was relieved to see his brother standing in the corner of the room, unharmed. "What on Earth happened?" Konstantin asked.

"Hitler is unwilling to stop his quest for control of the rest of Europe," Alexei said. "We had just finished our meeting when one of his guards tried to shoot me."

"Did he miss?" Konstantin asked. "You don't have a scratch on you."

"No, his aim was spot on," Alexei replied. "Gorvenko stepped in front of me."

Suddenly, Konstantin noticed that Alexei's ever-present, practically omniscient police chief was not in the room. "He didn't make it, did he?"

Alexei shook his head, and tears glistened in his eyes. His sons finally began crying, and he and Ileana hugged them.

Konstantin felt tears rolling down his own face as he looked at Igor. "You were supposed to protect Alyosha too," he said.

"I did," Igor replied indignantly, his voice rising. "I killed the Nazi guard who was firing at Alyosha, and I provided cover for him, Ileana and Kostya as they got out of the building."

"Igor could have been killed as easily as Gorvenko was," Alexei said, his voice shuddering.

Konstantin looked back at Igor. "I'm sorry," he said. "But the news was already reporting that Alyosha was killed. It was quite a shock."

Igor shook his head. "The Germans must have been spreading false rumors. Alyosha got out from under their noses. I'm sure they're embarrassed." He inhaled deeply, and Konstantin could see his chest starting to jut out. "Fuck the Nazis!" Igor suddenly bellowed, and Konstantin was almost knocked over by the force of his anger.

Vsevolod nodded. "That's goddamn right," he said. "I've wanted to fight the Axis powers since they funded Uncle Sandro's murder, and now they've almost killed Alyosha as well. We can't let this go unanswered. We Russians are not cowards!"

Konstantin grimaced. "So, what then?" he asked. "Another conflagration of war that will burn all of Europe to the ground?" *So much for fighting that war in Japan.*

Alexei sighed. "Much as the Great War horrified all of us, Kostya, I think we have no choice but to fight Hitler. He's evil, and he just took aim at us."

# DYNASTY IN HIDING

It was the beginning of March, 1941, and Konstantin could hear the winter wind screaming like a possessed spirit. *Two years of fighting the Nazis, and I'm not even sure we're winning,* he thought. He shivered even with his fur greatcoat wrapped around him, and he knew that his soldiers were suffering along with him. He pushed a pile of papers around in front of him, but even this simple task was made more difficult by the layers of gloves he wore. *At least we're getting reinforcements in the next day or two,* he thought as he examined the list of regiments that would be joining them.

Suddenly, Konstantin's heart jumped at the sight of the Chevalier Life Guards Regiment on the list. *That's Sevka's regiment,* he thought as he pictured his oldest nephew marching out when he had been deployed at the beginning of the war. Already, Konstantin felt as though the cold was lessening. *It would be great to see Sevka again. Ioann will be pleased to know that we've been reunited.*

When the Chevalier Life Guards Regiment stood in formation in front of Konstantin few days later, however, Vsevolod was nowhere to be seen. After inspecting the soldiers more than once to make sure that he really had not seen his nephew, Konstantin stopped in front of Major Avilov, the regiment's commanding officer. "Where is Vsevolod?" he asked as shells rained down nearby.

"Not here, sir," Avilov replied.

"Has he been injured or killed in action?"

"No, sir."

"Then where is he?"

Avilov's eyes moved to the men of his regiment, and Konstantin got the message. He dismissed the soldiers so that they could take up battle positions along the front and dragged Avilov off so that they could talk in private.

"Where is my nephew?" Konstantin demanded as soon as they were out of the rest of the regiment's earshot.

"On a secret mission for His Imperial Majesty," Avilov replied.

At the mention of Tsar Alexei II, Konstantin was so sure he had misheard Avilov that he stuck his fingers in his ears to see if there was any snow in them. When he was certain that they were clean, he asked, "what did you say?"

"His Serene Highness has not fought with this regiment since the war began."

"I saw him march off in your command a week after war was declared."

"And as soon as we were outside St. Petersburg, he left on whatever mission His Imperial Majesty had given him."

Konstantin glared at Avilov, and his blue eyes seemed to shoot snow and ice faster than the clouds above them. "Are you telling me Sevka's a spy?" he demanded. "Where has he been since the war began?"

"I really don't know, sir, you have to believe me," Avilov stuttered.

Konstantin continued glaring at him, and then something clicked in his mind. "Oh my God," he said, his eyes going from Avilov's face to the ground. His face suddenly felt warm despite the weather. "In the last few months, there's been talk of 'the Imperial Spy'- supposedly a member of the imperial family who's spying for the Russians, who's so good that the Germans have a price on his head."

Avilov nodded. "I'd bet anything it's Vsevolod. The soldiers in my regiment think it's him too, but I've forbidden them from talking about it, just in case they jeopardize his safety."

Konstantin looked back at him. "I always laughed when I heard those rumors because I thought they were ridiculous."

"Perhaps not."

Konstantin took a deep breath. "I'm sorry, Maxim Georgievich," he said finally. "But I really expected to see my nephew, and this is a bit of a shock."

"I understand, sir."

With a jerk of his head, Konstantin told Avilov to join his soldiers. Avilov saluted and disappeared. For a moment, Konstantin felt as though the world was spinning underneath him. Putting out his hand, he felt his away along the barracks wall until he found a door. When he was inside, he collapsed into a chair. *Sevka's a spy,* he thought, and the worry that he had previously felt for his nephew doubled. *The Germans are really after him,* he thought. *I wonder what he's done. I'm sure some of it has to do with his status as a Prince of the Imperial Blood, but even so, the Nazis wouldn't care about him to such an extent if he hadn't discovered some of their secrets.*

For several months, Konstantin tried to forget about what he suspected about Vsevolod. It was only after the portion of the army that was under his command had won the Battle of Sebastopol and he was being transferred to Smolensk, that Konstantin came closer to the truth. By then, it was December, and Konstantin felt no warmer than he had in March. Upon his arrival at Smolensk, the army was in flux. Several regiments that had been depleted were moving out, while others were transferring in. Only an hour after his arrival, Konstantin reviewed the troops, both the regiments that were leaving, and a few of the ones that had just arrived.

Konstantin marched in front of the line of soldiers, thanking them for their service and giving them words of encouragement. As he walked, he noticed several tall soldiers at the end of the row. *That was what Ioann and Gavril always looked like when lined up with their regiments*, he thought. His brothers' names were barely formed in his mind when he recognized the features of one of the tall soldiers. *Shit, it's Sevka!* he thought. *No wonder I thought of Ioann!*

But when Konstantin looked at both Vsevolod's uniform and the decorations on his chest, he had to control his anger. *His uniform is wrong, and he's a major in his regiment!* he nearly snarled. *What's he doing wearing the decorations of a goddamned private?*

Vsevolod continued to stare straight ahead as Konstantin finished his review. In an instant, Konstantin realized that Vsevolod had recognized him as well, but was maintaining his cover as a spy. He looked over at the commanding officer next to him and realized that in his surprise at seeing Vsevolod, he had forgotten the man's name. "Colonel," he said smoothly, covering his confusion, "I need to know what wisdom you've gleaned from fighting here these past few weeks."

"Absolutely, sir," the colonel replied. "Our train out of here doesn't leave for another hour."

"Then come with me, and let's bring a few of your soldiers, so that they may chime in as well." Konstantin gestured for a couple of the nearest soldiers, including Vsevolod, to follow them, and they began walking towards the barracks. Then he dismissed the rest of the soldiers in front of him.

Konstantin listened with interest as the colonel filled him in on the details of the recent fighting. He threw out a couple of questions for the enlisted men next to them. When they arrived at the barracks, Konstantin thanked them for their service. He shook hands with most of them, but made sure he was standing next to Vsevolod, and placed a hand at his back as he did. He pressed his hand against Vsevolod's back, hoping his nephew would understand the gesture, and thought he felt Vsevolod leaning backwards slightly into his hand.

Then, feeling as though he could not, in good conscience, hold the soldiers any longer, he dismissed them. The colonel and most of the men made a quick dash back to the rest of the regiment. Vsevolod followed at a fast pace, but he turned around long enough to make eye contact with Konstantin and give him a nod.

Konstantin nodded back, and tried to smile. "Good luck, Private," he said.

"Thank you, sir," Vsevolod responded. Then he turned away completely and followed the colonel in front of him.

Konstantin watched him until he could no longer see him. Then he turned and went to the base's command center, clenching his teeth so as not to let his tears overflow. *This damn war*, he thought. *I've just started counting down the days until it ends.*

# THE WAR COMES HOME

Konstantin felt the rough paper of the telegram he held in his hands. A fear of opening the telegram shuddered through him as the whine of guns and the Russian Imperial Air Force swirled around him. Konstantin took a deep breath, but it did little to banish the feeling of fear that sat on his chest like a heavy animal. Finally, Konstantin forced his fingers to open the missive. *Leaving the news unknown will not erase what's happened,* he thought.

When he finally wrenched the telegram open, Konstantin had to press the paper against a nearby table to read it- his hands were shaking so badly that the words in front of him were unintelligible. When his eyes finally scanned the message in front of him, Konstantin's insides curled like snakes. "Peter has been badly wounded at the front, is en route to a hospital here in St. Petersburg," the telegram said. Alexei's signature was scrawled at the bottom.

"Shit!" Konstantin yelped. *Igor's oldest son- he'd better survive.* Konstantin made arrangements for his army's leadership to be left in the hands of General Rokossovsky. Then he traveled back to the Russian capital as quickly as he could. Soon, he was feeling the cold March air through a tiny crack in the train car window as he traveled. *Please Petya, pull through this,* he thought. Despite his prayers, however, Konstantin could not keep out his memories of when he had traveled like this during the First World War, desperate to get back in time for the funerals of his father and brother.

As soon as his train arrived in St. Petersburg, Konstantin dashed for the hospital. When he arrived, Igor and Sophie were already sitting next to their son's bedside, and they didn't look happy. Their youngest son, Oleg, sat next to them, keeping an eye on his oldest brother. Alexei stood nearby, looking uneasy.

Konstantin looked at Peter and was frightened by how gray his skin looked. He went over to Igor and rested a hand on his shoulder. "How is he?" he asked, nodding at his nephew.

Igor looked at Peter and frowned. Then he looked at Konstantin and shook his head.

In that instant, Konstantin could tell that Igor didn't expect Peter to live. "What happened?" he asked.

"He was out on patrol when he met a Nazi advance force," Igor said.

Slowly, Peter turned his head towards Konstantin and Igor. "I shot at them too," he whispered.

"Did you hit any of them?" Konstantin asked.

"Kostya," Igor said, shaking his head.

"What?" Konstantin asked.

But Peter was nodding. "I killed one of their colonels," he said. "It made them real mad."

"I don't give a damn about a Nazi colonel, I care about my son," Igor said angrily, pushing back his chair and standing up.

Oleg eyed Igor, and Konstantin could see tears in Oleg's eyes.

"Relax, Igor," Konstantin said. "I think Petya will make it." *Actually, I'm not so sure. He looks really bad.*

Just then, Nicholas pulled himself in from the front, holding his huge sniper rifle. Konstantin was glad to see him, but he was startled by just how large his gun was. Nicholas looked at Peter. Then he looked at Igor and Sophie, and he bit his lip. "How are you feeling, Petya?" he asked as he lay down his gun.

"Never better," Peter said with a smile as he looked back at his younger brother.

"Liar," Nicholas replied, but he was smiling too.

After a few minutes, Peter drifted off to sleep, and Nicholas stepped out into the hallway to talk to Alexei. Konstantin watched him go, then looked back at Peter. Even in the few seconds that he'd been distracted, Peter's countenance seemed to have become grayer. Fearing the worst, Konstantin looked over at the nurse in the room, and she came hurrying over. When Konstantin looked back at Peter, he was no longer breathing. "I'm sorry," the nurse said, shaking her head.

Igor let out a wail that sounded like a banshee, and Konstantin felt like his whole body was sinking. Nicholas and Alexei raced back into the room. Already, Sophie and Oleg were crying. Alexei put his arm around Igor, and Konstantin hugged Oleg.

"I'm sorry," Konstantin said, struggling to talk around the lump that had arisen in his throat.

The funeral did little to comfort either Konstantin or Igor, both of whose tears flowed copiously, but to no avail. *All the pain in the world won't bring Petya back,* Konstantin thought. *This is how Papa must have felt when Oleg was killed in the first Great War.*

When the funeral was over, the family made its way back to Pavlovsk. As night fell, Konstantin realized that he would have to begin his journey back to the front in the morning. *Rokossovsky is an incredible general,* he thought, *and yet I must get back to the fighting. We need to defeat the Nazis, now more than ever.* When he looked around for Igor, however, his brother was nowhere to be seen.

"Are you looking for Igor?" Ioann asked. Konstantin nodded. "He just went upstairs."

*I guess I'm not the only one keeping an eye on him,* Konstantin thought as he boarded the stairs. *This is a terrible loss.* He headed for the apartments that Igor, Sophie and their kids shared when they stayed at Pavlovsk. He knocked at the door when he arrived at the apartments, but when there was no answer, he entered anyway. To his surprise, Igor wasn't in his bedroom.

Without hesitating, Konstantin made his way over to Peter's bedroom, and it was there that he found Igor, sitting on Peter's bed, staring out the window, tears flowing down his face. Konstantin went and sat next to his younger brother and took his hand. *I really don't know what to say. Igor lost one child before it was even born, and now he's lost his oldest son to the war. If I didn't know better, I'd think he was cursed entirely.* "I'm sorry," he said finally.

Igor didn't respond. Instead, he pulled his hand away from Konstantin's and wiped his running nose. Then he inhaled, and when he exhaled, his breath came out shuddering like an unstable wall in a high wind. "I'm cursed, Kostya," he said.

Feeling his words fail him once again, Konstantin simply reached out and pulled Igor to him into an embrace. *Either of my sons could be next,* he thought. *Or any of my other nephews.* He heard footsteps in the hall, and a second later, Nicholas and Oleg appeared in the doorway. Both of them came into the room, and Konstantin moved to let them sit next to Igor.

"We're going to defeat the Nazis, I swear, Papa," Nicholas said.

Igor shrugged hopelessly. "They've already beaten us in a lot of ways," he said.

Konstantin shook his head vehemently. "Our armies are strong, and we will not give up," he said. "We're going to wipe the Nazi scourge off the face of the Earth, one way or another."

"You'll see, Papa," Oleg added. "So much of our family is still fighting at the front. I'll bet anything it's we Romanovs who will march into Berlin and take Hitler down once and for all."

# FRESH WOUNDS IN WARTIME

It was the middle of December, 1941, and Konstantin shivered as he laid out maps in front of him, trying to decide where and when to make the next offensive. Suddenly, the phone in front of him jangled, and Konstantin jumped. "Hello?" he said a minute later, when his heart wasn't beating quite so fast.

"Kostya, it's Alyosha," Alexei said on the other end.

"Got any plans for a new offensive?" Konstantin asked. "I could use the inspiration."

For a second, Alexei hesitated on the other end, and even in that split second, Konstantin's insides filled with fear. "I'm sorry to have to give you this news, Kostya," Alexei said, "but Sergei's been wounded at the front."

"Shit!" Konstantin howled. "What happened?"

"His plane was shot down. He managed to eject, but apparently the landing was not a smooth one."

"Where is he now?"

"He was patched up a bit at the front, but he's being brought to a hospital here in St. Petersburg." Alexei gave him the name of the hospital.

Konstantin was silent for a moment as he thought about it. "I can make it back."

"Do you have officers that can cover for you?" Alexei asked. "I'd hate to see your gains against the Germans reversed."

"Don't worry, I have several colonels under me that I trust."

Konstantin had barely hung up the phone when he was making arrangements for a quick flight back to St. Petersburg. *We generals are only supposed to use these planes when we're going to meet with Alyosha or going to a different part of the front to lead the Army,* he thought. *I hate to have to make an exception because of the example it sets, but I do want to see Sergei before he…*

Konstantin swallowed as the plane took off. *Maybe he'll survive,* he thought. He stared out the window of the small plane, willing it to go faster. When he arrived at the hospital in St. Petersburg, Pilar was pacing around, tears streaming down her face, as Igor and Alexei tried to calm her down. Ioann and Elena and their daughters were there as well. Ileana also stood nearby, biting her lips.

Konstantin rushed over to Pilar and hugged her. Then his younger son, Boris, and his two daughters, Olga and Marie, raced into the hospital. The rest of Konstantin's siblings, nieces and nephews followed them. "Mama! Papa!" Boris yelped, dashing over to them. "Where's Sergei?"

"Still in surgery," Pilar replied. "The doctors are supposed to tell us when he's out." She hugged the rest of her children.

Konstantin could barely contain his tears.

Ioann shook his head. "First Petya, now this."

"You don't have to remind me," Konstantin said.

Ioann looked over at Alexei. "Vyacheslav has been writing regularly from the front, at least, but I haven't heard from Sevka in awhile," he said of his sons. "It really makes me worry."

"I just spoke to Sevka's commanding officer yesterday," Alexei reassured him. "He's fine."

Konstantin deliberately kept silent. *Ioann and Elena don't know that Sevka's a spy. Well, there's no way I'm telling them that.*

*Sevka would kill me, and anyway, he needs to maintain his cover.* Konstantin took a deep breath as he looked for one of the doctors, hoping for news of Sergei.

Behind him, Ioann continued to look at Alexei. "I'm just glad that Gleb hasn't been conscripted yet," he said of his youngest son. "But if this war goes on any longer, he will be."

Alexei was about to reply when one of the hospital's nurses approached the family. When she saw Konstantin, she said, "Your Serene Highness, your son is out of surgery."

Konstantin, Pilar, Boris, Olga and Marie went to Sergei's room as the rest of the family waited outside in the hallway. Inside the room, Konstantin sucked in a breath when he saw his son wrapped in casts and bandages. Sergei was lying on his bed, one leg and one arm in casts. His whole midsection was wrapped in bandages, and he winced slightly at every breath he took. "Dammit," Konstantin spat.

"Relax, Papa," Sergei replied. "I'm alive, and I killed a bunch of Germans even as my plane went down."

Pilar took Sergei's hand as her tears continued to flow. The nurse in the room eyed Konstantin and Pilar. "Your son's a fighter," she said. "Given his injuries, I'm amazed he made it to the hospital alive, and when he got here, he was still yelling his head off."

Pilar almost smiled at that, but Konstantin fixed his translucent eyes on the nurse in a glowering stare. "Does that mean he'll definitely survive?" he asked.

"Yes, all the doctors that treated him think so."

"See, Papa?" Sergei said. "All that worrying for nothing."

Konstantin shook his head at his son. After a few more minutes of talking to Sergei, mostly to reassure himself at his son's safety, Konstantin stuck his head into the hall and looked at the rest of the family. "He's awake," he said.

In the hall, Alexei and Ileana waited for Konstantin's siblings, nieces and nephews to go in before following them. Sergei was clearly in pain, but he smiled when he saw the rest of the family, and Konstantin almost felt reassured.

"God, Gega," Ioann said. "What happened?"

"The Germans shot me down," Sergei replied. "I managed to bail out before I crashed. Luckily I landed behind Russian lines."

"I don't think this will go down as one of your better landings," Konstantin said pointedly.

Sergei rolled his eyes at his father. "It could have been worse. Besides, my burning plane landed smack in the middle of a German tank division, and a lot of explosions followed. I couldn't have aimed better if I'd tried." He grinned.

Boris, Olga and Marie grinned back at him. Konstantin, looking at the rest of the family, saw that everyone else was smiling too.

# A LIFETIME OF SERVICE

Another war was over, and once again Konstantin was taking the train back to St. Petersburg. He stared out the window, feeling claustrophobic and trying to ignore the number of soldiers that were packed in around him. *Most of these men are under my command,* he thought. *This would be unbearable otherwise.*

He thought of when the first World War had ended. *We had to change trains in Lvov. It was snowing then, and I met Ioann's regiment on the platform.* Now, though, it was summertime, and the heat of the train car was exacerbated by the flies that buzzed around Konstantin's head. Konstantin swung at the fly near his nose, and succeeded in pushing it up against the window before killing it. The men around him cheered, and Konstantin smiled. "Almost as easy as killing the Nazis," he said. The comment produced another round of cheers.

"Your Serene Highness, is it true that the Heir to throne killed Hitler?" a major standing next to Konstantin asked when the cheers died down.

"I've heard the same rumors you have," Konstantin admitted. "But I've been as far away from the capital as you have." *I may be a general and a member of the imperial family, but I definitely wasn't a part of Alyosha's decision-making on that one.* Seeing the rest of the men's interested eyes on him, Konstantin added, "I find it incredible that the Tsar would send his oldest son a mission like that, but I'm going to be the first one off this train when it gets into St. Petersburg, so I'll find out before any of you do."

The men laughed, and Konstantin felt a certain amount of pride swell within him. *Nearly half the family has been fighting in this war,* he thought. Once his soldiers' attention was off him, Konstantin continued retreating into his own head, thinking about whether those rumors could possibly be true. *A Russian bomb killed Hitler, that much we all know,* he thought. *Still, the thought that Kostya delivered that bomb and got caught up in the Battle of Berlin as he fled the Reichstag is too much for me to believe.*

Konstantin looked out the window again, watching the scenery fly by and feeling the rocking of the train car. *I can't wait to see Pilar and the kids again,* he thought. *I hope Sergei's almost healed from his injuries. I wonder if Boris has made it back from the front yet.*

Konstantin clenched his teeth, willing his tears to stay hidden. *When I came home from the last Great War, it was as a son whose father had died and whose brother had been killed in action. Now I'm the father whose son was wounded and whose nephew was killed in action.* The mere thought of Peter's funeral, and of Igor's pain, sent Konstantin's tears down his face, and he stared resolutely out the window, praying that the men around him didn't see him crying.

When his face was dry, Konstantin stared at his feet, seeing the dust on his feet and feeling how worn his boots were. *Our armies may have been victorious yet again, but enough is enough. I'm done with war and all it entails.* He took a deep breath and felt a weariness that cut into him like a cold winter wind.

When the train pulled into St. Petersburg, Konstantin could hear the cheers of the people waiting on the platform, and he smiled despite himself. *Pilar and the children better be among the people waiting,* he thought. *Or they won't hear the end of it.*

Konstantin shook his head at himself as the train came to a complete stop. *The children are adults,* he thought. *Boris and Sergei have been risking their lives at the front, the same as I have, and Sergei almost got killed for it.* He took a deep breath as he disembarked, and saw Alexei standing at attention, welcoming the soldiers back. Right next to him, his heir, another Konstantin, also stood saluting, but his left arm was in a sling. *Shit,* Konstantin thought. *Those rumors must have been true. Unbelievable.*

Konstantin hadn't even realized that he had snapped into a salute until Alexei dismissed the soldiers. He grinned as he hugged the tsar, then hugged Konstantin. "What happened to you?" he demanded as the sixteen-year-old grimaced.

"I got shot on the way out of Berlin," the younger Konstantin replied.

"So everything that I've been hearing is true? You and your bomb killed Hitler?" Konstantin let out a string of curses as his younger cousin nodded, grinning, obviously proud of himself. Konstantin shook his head at Alexei. "I can't believe you sent him straight into the lion's den."

"It seems crazier now in retrospect, even though it worked out," Alexei replied, and Konstantin saw a combination of regret and pride in his eyes.

Then Konstantin heard his brothers calling him, and without warning, Ioann, Gavril, Igor and George piled on top of him, hugging him. Konstantin hugged them all back, feeling like his heart was going to come out of his chest with happiness. *I'm home,* he thought. *I'm home, safe and sound.*

When his brothers piled off him, Konstantin saw that Vsevolod was right behind Ioann, and he hugged him tightly as well. "Sevka," he said. "It's good to be able to say I know you." They both laughed.

"If you'd broken my cover, though, that would have been the end of it," Vsevolod admitted seriously.

Ioann eyed them.

"I ran into Sevka at the front," Konstantin told his oldest brother. "He was undercover, though, so I had to pretend he was just some soldier."

Ioann shook his head, and his eyes glistened with tears. "Did you know I spent most of the war thinking he was at the front with his regiment? I didn't know he was a spy until Alyosha was making plans to send him to Berlin with Kostya."

Konstantin put one arm around Ioann's shoulders, the other around Vsevolod's. "Sounds like you have a lot to catch up on."

Ioann nodded. "We've had a few days since he and Kostya got back, but it hasn't been enough time yet."

"These things take awhile," Konstantin said. He looked at Vsevolod. "I'd be interested in hearing your stories too. Maybe you should write your memoirs."

Vsevolod laughed. "I'll do it when I'm old and there's nothing else for me to do with my life."

Konstantin shook his head. "To the contrary, you should do it before you forget everything."

Then another train pulled into the station, and Boris and Nicholas were among the soldiers that poured off the train. "Nicky!" Igor howled, and Nicholas dove into his father's arms.

Konstantin grinned as he embraced Boris. *One son wounded at the front, the other one home safely*, he thought, smiling as Boris, Nicholas and Vsevolod cracked jokes. "Where's the rest of the family?" Boris asked.

"We had to evacuate them from the city," Ioann replied. "But they should be on one of these trains back."

Boris looked at Konstantin and shook his head. "We're off fighting at the front and still our family isn't safe in the capitol?"

"This was a tough battle, Boris," Konstantin said. "The Nazis made it as far as Moscow and St. Petersburg." *But I agree with him. I know what I was fighting for, and still I question fighting if my family wasn't safe.*

Even thinking of the war again made Konstantin feel the crush of people on the station's platform. He was glad to home, happy to reunited with his family, and yet…

Konstantin took a deep breath. *I'd give anything for some open space, and some quiet,* he thought. *I could be back at Strelna in minutes.* The thought of his palace made Konstantin long for the comforts of home. *If the whole family were here, we'd be on our way to Strelna already,* he thought impatiently.

Finally, another train pulled into the station. Konstantin heard Alexei yell, "Ileana!" He looked through the windows of the train and could see the Tsarina waving furiously. Her younger children surrounded her, jumping up and down. They dashed off the train as soon as it stopped, and a second later, Konstantin saw Pilar stepping off the train as well. Olga, Marie and Sergei were right behind her. Konstantin's heart jumped for joy, and he dove at his wife. "Pilar!" he yelped. "I'm home!"

"So am I!" she cried back as they threw their arms around each other.

Then Konstantin hugged Olga and Marie as Boris embraced Sergei. "How are you feeling?" Konstantin asked Sergei. *He's still limping and using his crutches. I'm worried that his injuries may never heal properly.*

But Sergei's words were reassuring. "I'm a lot better," he said. "We had a hell of a time evacuating from the city, but I've been recovering since then."

"What happened?" Boris asked, and Konstantin felt himself shivering slightly, almost afraid to hear the answer.

"The Germans bombed us as we went. The train derailed!"

"Oh my God!" Konstantin clapped his hand to his forehead. "It's incredible you made it out of there alive!"

"Mostly because of the help of this guy!" Sergei said with a grin as he reached out and pulled his cousin Oleg into a hug. Of course, Oleg's back was to Sergei, so his arm went around Oleg's shoulder and neck.

"Help!" Oleg yelped, throwing up his arms as he was dragged backwards towards Sergei. But both he and Sergei were laughing, and Igor, standing next to his youngest son, joined them.

Later that night, Konstantin walked down one of the long hallways of Strelna. He heard his boots click on the parquet floors, and he felt the silence around him as though it hung in the air like water droplets. For a moment, he stood still, closed his eyes, and took a deep breath. He stood like that for a second breath, and then a third, wishing he could inhale the silence until it was a part of his body and quieted the turmoil inside of him.

*War,* Konstantin thought. *It never gets any easier. I thought World War I was brutal, but the Nazis were beyond my worst imagination.*

He opened his eyes and was glad for the familiar hallway. Another deep breath began to quiet his churning stomach, and still he couldn't stop the torrent of thoughts that were flooding his brain. *I've spent my whole life training for war,* he realized. *It's time to end that cycle.*

Konstantin heard footsteps behind him, and turned to see his family coming down the hall. Pilar, her blond hair finally streaked with gray, supported Sergei. Next to him, Boris, still wearing his uniform, also supported his older brother, but he was smiling. Olga and Marie followed, standing on their tiptoes to see if their father was indeed down the hallway.

Konstantin smiled and walked towards them. *It's so good to be home, back in the company of the people that matter to me most.* He could see Pilar's eyes searching his as he embraced each member of the family. "What are you thinking, Kostya?" she asked.

Konstantin looked at his wife, and then at each of their children. "I have been a military man my whole life," he said. "And yet this war brought me to the edge of my humanity. It's time to retire."

Marie and Olga looked stunned, but Sergei and Boris were nodding. "I remember how excited I was to go off to war," Sergei said. "But it's nothing I would ever do again."

Pilar looked at her husband and smiled. "All those years you spent training, and all those years you spent fighting- I spent each and every minute of it wishing we could be together. Now we'll have the time to do just that."

# TAMING THE GHOSTS OF THE PAST

Konstantin, kneeling, placed one last book in his trunk and slammed the lid closed with a bang. Then he put his hands on the top of the trunk and pushed himself up, groaning as he stood. *My knees have been killing me for weeks,* he thought. He was still wincing when Pilar came into the room. "What's bothering you?" she asked.

"My knees," Konstantin replied, struggling to replace his pained look with a smile. "But at least I'm all packed."

"I am too," Pilar said, the beginnings of a smile making her lips curl upward. "It's so nice that we've been able to travel."

Konstantin nodded. "Retirement has its perks, and the warm climates have really been wonderful in the winter," he agreed. "I've always loved the Crimea, and the fact that we've maintained a palace there has made life worthwhile."

Pilar laughed. "I'm not complaining, either, but I've always loved the mountains, too," she said.

"Of course you do. You're from Bavaria. It's always been beautiful there as well. It's why we're headed back there now."

Pilar's smile faded, and her fingers picked at the sweater she was holding. "I've always dreamed of going back there," she said. "And yet it's changed so much since I was a child that I wonder what I've been holding onto my memories for."

Konstantin took his wife's elbow and led her to the room's overstuffed couch. Together, they sat down. "I can't deny that Bavaria has changed, even since the time we met- and we were adults then," Konstantin said. "But it is still your homeland, and I want to return there with you."

Pilar stood up and went to the window, dropping her sweater onto the top of Konstantin's trunk as she did so. "Germany started both World War I and World War II," she said. "The Nazis considered Bavaria their second home. I don't know that I can feel the same way about a place that has harbored so much evil."

Konstantin followed his wife to the window. "I understand your fears," he said. "But Bavaria's physical beauty is still there- its snow-capped mountains, its wildflowers. Maybe you can keep your heart open as we return there."

Pilar stared out the window for another minute. Then she took a deep breath and looked at her husband. "It certainly couldn't hurt to try," she said.


When they drove up to their Bavarian hotel a week later, Konstantin could see the towering mountains in the distance. He took a deep breath as he and Pilar stepped out of the car and could smell the alpine freshness of the mountain air. On the other side of the car, he could see Pilar doing the same. "Aaahhh," she said. "At least the air smells the same as I remember it."

Konstantin smiled at her as the hotel's porters came out to help them unload their trunks from the car. "See?" he said. "There are still some things that are as they were in our youth."

For the next several days, they spent as much time outside as they could. It was on a hike through the mountains that Konstantin finally felt the mountains' peace seeping into his bones. *No military parades, no soldiers to review,* he thought. *That's all I'd be doing if I were still working.*

For a minute, Konstantin closed his eyes. He could feel the cool breeze float through his hair, and he could smell the trees around him. Then he felt Pilar take his hand. When he opened his eyes, he saw that his wife, who had initially stopped a distance behind him to continue looking at the mountains through a break in the trees, had now caught up to him. "Feeling better?" he asked, wondering if his wife's fears about visiting her homeland had smoothed out at all.

"I think so," Pilar said. She looked back up the path behind them, then back at Konstantin. "Did you know that my brothers and I used to go hiking on this very path?" she asked. "Our father joined us occasionally when he could get away from performing surgery at the hospital."

"I'm glad you have such good memories of your homeland," Konstantin said. "Do you still feel like the intervening wars and other evil have tainted them, though?"

"A little bit," Pilar admitted, moving out of the way of a young couple that was coming up the path.

Konstantin eyed the couple as they passed, remembering when he and Pilar had been that young couple, walking alongside the Seine River one winter evening. Then he looked back at his wife. "I understand your pain," he said. "I've fought in two world wars to defeat that evil, and my combat memories will always be with me."

"But?" Pilar said, certain that her husband had some other point to make.

"*But* I'd hate to see that turn into a self-imposed exile from your homeland. If your father's lifespan is any indication, you too may still have several decades of life in front of you. I wouldn't want you to feel as though you had to spend it separated from Bavaria." Konstantin shook his head as he eyed the trees around them once more. "I don't think I could bear to be separated from Russia for so long. I don't think I could go live somewhere else permanently, without the option of ever returning."

Pilar took a deep breath as she contemplated Konstantin's advice. "Don't worry," she said. "I haven't given up on Bavaria entirely."

# FINAL ENDINGS

Twenty years after the end of World War II, Konstantin lay ill. For days now, a lung ailment had racked his chest, and the disease had come on so quickly that his doctors could not even advise him to move to a warmer climate in the hopes of improving. *Who needs a warmer climate anyway, when it's August in St. Petersburg?* Konstantin wondered. *The weather is beautiful.*

Konstantin looked out the window, glad that the sun was rising, a fiery orange globe set against a deep blue sky. *I haven't slept well since I became ill,* he thought. *All I do is cough and sweat, unless I'm shivering.* Konstantin looked back out the window, but even turning his head towards the window tired him out, and he groaned. *I'm seventy-one years old,* he thought. *I've had a long and full life, and yet…*

*I don't know,* Konstantin thought. *I wish I were young again. I miss riding a horse. I miss being healthy.*

The sound of a chair being scraped against the floor distracted him, and Konstantin turned to see Pilar sitting next to him. Her hair was gray now rather than blond, and lines streaked her face. "I'm sorry I kept you up most of the night," Konstantin said.

"It's not a problem," Pilar responded. "Sleep is never easy when you're ill."

Konstantin smiled. "I still remember how you came to see me right before our wedding ceremony, when we weren't supposed to see each other until the ceremony began. If anyone had found out you did that, they would have called off the wedding then and there."

Pilar smiled in return. "I still don't regret it," she said.

"You were always the rebel."

"This from the man who changed the seating at a huge royal wedding so that your bachelor brothers could sit next to eligible princesses."

Konstantin laughed, but the laugh quickly turned into a hacking cough. Pilar handed him a handkerchief, and Konstantin felt its rough linen as he pressed it against his lips. When he could breathe again, he shook his head. "What a way to die," he said. "I always assumed it be from a bullet- quick and painless."

"Don't talk like that," Pilar whispered.

Konstantin heard the sound of the door being opened, and he managed to turn his head enough to see Sergei and Boris creep into the room. He smiled at them, and the smile widened when he saw Sergei's oldest son, Peter, behind them. "How are you feeling, Papa?" Sergei asked.

"Never better," Konstantin replied, despite the weakness that he felt in his chest and limbs. He looked at Peter. "How is your training going?"

"It's going well, Apapa," Peter replied.

Pilar smiled at her husband. "Always the military man," she said.

"You knew that when you married me," Konstantin said.

At noon, Pilar brought Konstantin some hot broth, and he swallowed it gratefully as he listened to the chimes of the grandfather clock in the hallway. Sergei, Boris and Peter had already left the room, so once the clock stopped speaking, it became very quiet.

Konstantin took a deep breath and found himself appreciating his palace's tranquility. His eyelids began to feel very heavy, and his chest began to feel as though something large were sitting on it. As Konstantin glanced around the room one last time, he noticed that the walls looked like they were bathed in a gray twilight.

Then, as the silence descended like a weighted felt curtain, Prince Konstantin Konstantinovich Romanov closed his eyes for the last time.

# ABOUT THE AUTHOR

*Through the Fire* is Tamar Anolic's first collection of short stories. Several of her short stories have been published individually in "The Copperfield Review," "The Helix," and "The Sandy River Review." She is also the author of *The Russian Riddle*, the first published biography of the Grand Duke Sergei Alexandrovich of Russia. Tamar's second novel, *Triumph of a Tsar*, is also about the Romanovs; *Through the Fire* is set in the same alternate historical universe as *Triumph of a Tsar*. Tamar's first novel is entitled *The Last Battle*.

www.ingramcontent.com/pod-product-compliance
Lightning Source LLC
Chambersburg PA
CBHW061502050726

47593CB00002B/416